GO WEST

DIVORAN LITES

CHAPTER 1

ELLIE

Elizabeth Morgan, looked out the train window at a sign that said, Clifton Colorado. It was here she hoped to find a plan and purpose for her new life. As the train drew to a stop, she stood and picked up her violin case. Smoothing kiss curls over each cheek, she straightened her narrow-brimmed cloche. She reached toward the shelf for her tapestry bag, and a long arm reached over her head and carefully lifted it down. She looked up into the eyes of tall man with silver-blond hair. He held the carpetbag in one hand and a deep brown Boss of the Prairie Stetson in the other. She didn't know yet who he was, but she knew from working in her grandparents' department store back home, that he had good taste in hats. His frayed khaki shirt, however, looked as if it were part of a uniform from the Great War.

"Name's Aldon Leitzinger, Miss Morgan. The conductor told me you were in this car." Warmth and an out-door fragrance radiated from his gangly frame as he stepped into the aisle and started moving away. Ellie hurried to throw her camel hair cape over her arm and follow.

"Are you from Spruce Creek Ranch?" she asked. He paused to toss an answer over his shoulder.

"Yes, ma'am. I'm foreman there." He moved on. When he got to the exit, he jumped two feet down onto the boardwalk and turned to help her. She hesitated and before she could discern his intention he jammed the hat on his head and snaked an arm around her to lift her down and deposit her on the boardwalk. Her stylish half-boots boots wobbled on the uneven platform.

"Whoa there." He steadied her. "Don't worry, you'll soon get used to the altitude." He put a hand under her elbow, but she shook him off.

"It's not the altitude. I wasn't ready; that's all." She had meant to be courteous, but she found herself irritated by this confident manner.

"You're as scrappy as a banty hen, aren't you?" He grinned.

"What is the altitude here, anyway?" she asked to cover her outrage at his arrogance.

"Right here we're over eight thousand feet above sea-level." He started walking toward the station house and she stepped quickly over the uneven boards trying to keep up. He pointed at a range of mountains in the distance. "The ranch is at ten-thousand feet and some of those peaks go up to fourteen thousand. What's the altitude in Chicago, Miss Morgan?"

So he knew not only her name, but where she had come from. Maybe as foreman he'd read her curriculum vitae. No harm in that. She knew she'd been hired not for the words on a slip of paper, but mainly because of Granddad's love of the West and because he knew the man who leased the ranch.

"Five hundred eighty-six feet." Fortunately, Granddad had read that statistic to her from the morning paper before she left their home in Chicago five days ago

"Did you bring any more baggage?" He stopped at a wooden bench outside the office and motioned for her to sit down.

"A trunk," she said.

"Okay, I'll be a minute." Setting down the carpetbag, he strode off toward the last cars on the train. She was deep in thought when he returned with her Douglas Vulcanized Wardrobe Trunk on his shoulder. He bent his knees to pick up the carpetbag and was off again.

"Those mountains are beautiful," Ellie said as they stepped onto the sidewalk that lined one side of the only block of Main Street.

"That's the Sangre de Cristo range." He reminded her of Cooper

Randolph, her favorite western movie star. Before she left home, Granddad had taken her to see him in "The End of the Trail," at the converted Palace Theater, which only a few years ago had been dedicated to burlesque.

"The name means blood of Christ. You see how the snow turns reddish as the sun goes down?" I heard pride and tenderness in his voice. Are you hungry?"

"Yes, we had to get back on the train before our luncheon arrived in Pueblo. I paid in advance, too." That still rankled. She believed in fairness in business.

"The springboard's at the livery here on Main Street. We'll be at the ranch in half an hour. Molly can give you some supper, and she won't make you pay first, either."

The broad gravel street still held faux-front buildings even though it was already 1924. To Ellie, the town looked old and shabby. Several farm wagons with their teams of horses were lined up on one side of the wide street. On the other side, she saw turn of the century motor cars angled toward the buildings.

Mr. Leitzinger carried her baggage into a livery stable full of warm animal smells and dust motes. On her left, a dappled gray horse thrust its long nose over a stall door and Ellie stepped back a pace.

"Do you ride?" Mr. Leitzinger inquired.

"Do I have to?"

"Most ranch hands do ride. Besides, horses are mighty fine creatures once you get to know them." He opened the half-door of the stall and pulled the big horse out by its halter. "Pardon me for saying so, ma'am, but you don't look much like a ranch hand."

"Oh, I can do anything I set my mind to." She said eyeing the horse warily. "Besides, I'm not a ranch hand. I'm supposed to help the housekeeper and act as lady's maid to the woman of the house."

"Evenin', Aldon," A man wearing suspenders over a long-sleeved undershirt walked out of the livery office. "Who's this purty lady?"

"Miss Elizabeth Morgan." Mr. Leitzinger put extra emphasis on the Miss. "She's our new ranch hand."

Ellie choked and started coughing. Those words reminded her that if she were to fail here, she'd report straight back to Grandmother to work in the department store beauty salon again. Once there, she'd give haircuts and machine waves until such time as Grandmother could find the proper husband for her. He would be a man so politically adept that he would end up in the governor's mansion with Ellie as wife and chatelaine. A cold shiver passed through her at the thought of it.

CHAPTER 2

ELLIE

"How do, ma'am." You don't look much like a ranch hand," the livery owner said.

Ellie opened her mouth to tell him she could handle about anything but the entrance of a young man captured her attention.

"This is Kenny, Donald Fitzgerald's son" Mr. Leitzinger said.

"How do, ma'am," Kenny touched his forehead and dipped his head. In Chicago a man would tip his hat as a sign of respect. She nodded in return.

"You'll have to hold Ribbons back," the boy spoke to Mr. Leitzinger. "She'll break into a run the first chance she gets. "Excuse me, ma'am." He moved past Ellie and reached for the halter and then backed the horse to the wagon which sat in the stable's alley. While Aldon stowed the luggage amongst other parcels, Kenny got the horse into harness.

"You might want to put your cape on, Miss Morgan." Mr. Leitzinger took the satin-lined garment from her arm, opened it, and settled it over her shoulders. She sighed as the heavy cloak warmed her. Capes had been a godsend in the ambulance corps. They protected the women drivers from the cold during the daytime and added extra blanketing at night. They could also be used to staunch blood, and for privacy when changing clothes.

Mr. Leitzinger watched as she pulled her doeskin gloves from the pockets of her cape and smoothed them over her fingers one by one. He looked away when she lifted her eyes to question his stare.

He got up on the narrow seat where the boy handed him the reins. "Put your foot on the axle-bolt and give me your hand," he told Ellie. As he hauled her up by one arm, Mr. Fitzgerald stepped forward and boosted her bottom as if she were a sack of goods. The men were so matter-of-fact about the process that she didn't bother to be embarrassed.

"Take hold of that bar under the seat until we get out on the road," Mr. Leitzinger suggested. She groped and felt the cold of the springy steel through her glove.

To her dismay, Mr. Leitzinger handed the reins to her while he reached for a leather jacket amongst the packages in the back. When he had shoved his arms into the sleeves, he took the reins again. A clucking noise urged the big gray forward and the wagon moved out of the shed.

"You didn't pay the liveryman," Ellie reminded him looking back to see if anyone was coming after them. In her grandparent's store anyone who didn't pay for services rendered was a lowlife. She hoped this cowboy person did not fall into that category.

"It's all right, Mr. Solano has me bring him to town once a month so he can pay the bills. At first he never left the ranch, but he's getting better now."

"Has he been ill?" she asked with a pang of anxiety. Surely they wouldn't expect her to add nursing to her other duties. She had developed such an aversion to pain and suffering she couldn't even listen to war stories without weeping.

"Signor Solano came to Colorado to get cured of his tuberculosis, and he is getting well." As he spoke, Mr. Leitzinger pulled back slightly on the reins.

"I thought TB was incurable," said Ellie.

"People do get well here," he answered. "It's the clean, dry air and the good food. They might have to stay a few years, and it's important to take it easy, but a cure is possible. Signor Solano feels that the oranges he orders trained in from California and Florida help.

They headed toward the snow-topped mountain peaks to the west passing several small houses that looked as if they had grown out of the surrounding land. "Those belong to our family," he said. "The settlers around here started with log cabins. When they prospered in the cattle business, they built big houses closer to the range. Most family members worked the ranches, but when they got old they sometimes moved to town. We have strong families here. Strong families make strong countries, or so I believe. What do you think?"

"I'm in favor of families, though sometimes you have to get away from them," Ellie said. What she didn't say was that she was also in favor of as much independence as possible.

"It takes guts to leave, but it feels good to come back home," said Mr. Leitzinger. "Signor Solano's grandson is coming from Switzerland tomorrow. We graded the road especially for his visit. It's a good thing the spring thaw is over. Water rushes through the canyons when the creeks flood and it can destroy the roads and the railroad tracks. A gully-washer has taken the tracks out twice.

"I know what you're saying, the roads in France were awful in winter and spring. As they were sitting shoulder to shoulder she appreciated the warmth radiating from his tall frame.

As the horse settled into a steady pace, Mr. Leitzinger handed Ellie the reins again. She held them tightly, hoping Ribbons wouldn't take a notion to bolt.

Mr. Leitzinger pulled a mouth-harp from his jacket pocket and cupped it in his hands beginning to play "It's a Long Way to Tipperary." Ellie hummed along. It was a song she knew from singing with ambulatory patients and off-duty nurses. At those times, she felt as if she were with family members even though they might never meet again.

"That's a flier's jacket, isn't it? Were you in the war?" she asked.

"The Great War. People don't want to think we'll ever have another one." He slid the harmonica back into his pocket and re-possessed the reins.

"No sane person wants a war," she shivered at the thought of another one.

"I wanted to be in the thick of the dog-fighting," he said. "But they needed men who could read maps and memorize terrain, so they taught me to fly and put me in a surveillance bus instead. A BeBe. That's a pretty good little airplane. My brother was in the infantry, but he didn't make it back home."

"Oh, I'm so sorry." She felt the sting of tears at the back of her eyes and dreaded the crying she felt approaching. After the war ended, she had spent five years in the beauty salon falling apart every time a patron told her a sad story.

Without saying anything further, Mr. Leitzinger shrugged, handed her the reins and took out his harmonica again. He breathed into the instrument and snappy Dixieland jazz emerged.

The lively tune distracted and soothed her. Now she wouldn't have to make a fool of herself with her tears.

The wagon turned and dipped under a wooden entrance with hieroglyphics burned into it.

"Is that your ranch brand?" she asked.

"How do you know about brands?" He stopped playing.

"My grandfather was raised on a ranch out here, and he always wanted to come back. He'd tell any callers who came to the house, 'Go West, young man and grown up with the country.'" He got that from a man named Horace Greely. I'm Granddad's first convert, even though I'm not a man."

"We'll have to invite him for a visit," Mr. Leitzinger said.

"On your sign, I saw an L…? She glanced back, but they were on the other side by now.

"Circle L-Z," he said. "That's our family brand, but we're leasing to Mr. Solano for the time being.

They drew up to a large Victorian house with windows across each of three floors. The lights on the ground floor issued a welcome. Large spruce trees grew as tall as the house on both sides.

CHAPTER 3

ALDON

As Ribbons pulled the wagon through the open door, Aldon glanced at his Flivver, which was up on blocks at the back of the barn. It was now springtime and he wanted to get it ready to drive to church the next day. That beloved grandson of Signor Solano's would arrive at noon. *Someday, we'll have roads we can drive our autos on in the winter. Right now the snow is too deep, the road gets icy, and the hills seem to run straight up.* Aldon sighed. *Someday.* His own flivver spent the winter on the leeward side of the barn covered with a tarpaulin. He hoped he could bring it back to life once he got the time to try. He had winterized both vehicles, drained the gasoline and the water and put them up on blocks. That was all he knew to do. Now, with so many people coming around they might need both autos.

"If you don't mind, you can take a seat on that hay bale while I put Ribbons up. We'll have supper in the kitchen, and I'll come back and get the automobiles ready to run us to church in the morning." He helped Miss Morgan down.

"I'd be glad to assist you," she said.

Reaching for the lantern and turning up the wick, Aldon avoided answering. He'd never thought about a woman working on a motor before. It didn't seem proper somehow.

She sat where he indicated while he removed the traces,

currycombed Ribbons, and checked her feet for gravel stones. Glancing over at Miss Morgan, he saw that her that shadowed her eyes but showed off the rest of her in the lamp-light. She had raspberry lips, a pert nose, and a purposeful chin. Her complexion looked delicate. He should get her into a real hat, if he could. *We're close to the sun at this altitude,* he thought, wondering whether she would consent to wear a sunbonnet or not. He then recalled his brother, Bill, with Grandma's homemade shade hat on his head backwards. The strings hung down over his face. Aldon chuckled.

"Is something funny?" Miss Morgan asked looking up. The light from the lantern turned her eyes into sparkling sapphires like the ones he'd seen at a museum in one those big cities in Europe.

"I'm thinking about my brother, he's a real clown."

"In the circus?" She had fine teeth when she smiled. If she had been a horse, he'd count them and see how old she was. His guess would be that she was about the same as him.

"No, ma'am, but he makes us laugh. Right now, he's a Hollywood-land stuntman and horse-wrangler for the moving pictures shows."

"I love the movies," Miss Morgan said. "Before I left, Granddad and I saw Cooper Randolph in 'Colt 45.'" She tilted her head: "You remind me of him."

"Your granddad?" he asked, teasing.

"No, not him, the movie star," she said.

"Well, what does this Cooper Randolph fellow do in the movies?" he asked.

"He gets rid of the bad guys." Miss Morgan stood and waited until he retrieved her carpetbag from the wagon.

"Do you need anything else for tonight?" he asked.

She shook her head, then inquired, "Was your brother in the war, too?"

"No ma'am, he had a heart murmur. We couldn't believe it. He always ran circles around the rest of us." Aldon took her arm and guided her over the straw-littered floor.

"Who lives up at the house?" She asked as they left the barn.

"Signor and Signora Solano and Molly," He opened the back gate.

"Not you?" She walked through as if somebody was always opening gates for her.

"I've moved into the loft for the summer." On the enclosed back porch, he pulled a string hanging from a light fixture. Wiring the house had been easy once he figured out how to harness the creek for power.

"Take off your coat and hat and stay awhile. That's what my family says when company comes." He helped Miss Morgan out of her cape and hung it on the peg Molly had cleared. The other pegs held coats, jackets, and dusters from the past two generations of ranchers. He liked having them there because they reminded him of family members who had gone to be with the Lord. Besides, they could be useful even now. A row of galoshes and boots sat lined up, ready for work. No need to buy new ones while these were still good.

Miss Morgan took off her hat and handed it to him. Now he could see that her hair was palomino blond. She smoothed curls over her cheeks while he placed the hat on the shelf where he knew his grandmother's sunbonnet lived. When they entered the kitchen, he breathed in the smell of a simmering stew.

"So this is a ranch kitchen," Miss Morgan looked around at the refractory table, the steel counters, and the blue enameled stove.

"Yep, that stove has been here since 1900, but it's a good one. It uses coal or wood. Ma used it until she moved to town. I sure missed her cooking, but then Molly moved in. She loves the stove, wouldn't use any other.

He pulled out a chair at the long table so she could watch the few lights glimmering in the valley below.

"What a lovely view," she said resting back with a sigh.

"So you can fix cars, huh?" he asked keeping a straight face.

"You read my letter of application?" she spoke slowly, and he nodded. "Well, wouldn't it stand to reason that if I can drive an ambulance, I can maintain and repair an engine and change tires? Who do you think, did all that?"

"You?" He turned and got her a glass of water out of the spigot. The ranch water came from the mountains and was cold, and delicious. She drank the whole glass as though she hadn't been watered since Illinois.

"I'll get Molly," he said.

When he reached the second floor, He heard soft voices coming from the Solano rooms. At least they weren't fighting for once. He hated the way the young Mrs. yelled at her husband. That white-haired man was old enough to be her father, if not her grandfather. He was the kindest and gentlest man Aldon had ever known. He walked on past to Molly's door, tapped and waited.

"You took your sweet time," Molly said yanking the door open. She wore a clean apron over her wash-dress, a sign she was ready for company. A crease ran down her cheek which showed she'd been napping, or as she called it, *resting her eyes*. In her opinion, only lazy people took naps.

CHAPTER 4

ALDON

"**S**ure'n you took your time, Aldon," Molly said in the Irish brogue she picked up from her family. She rubbed the bridge of her nose where her glasses usually rested. Aldon slipped into the room to find them for her before she asked.

"The missus screamed her head off at poor, dear Mr. Solano all evening," Molly said, putting on the glasses Aldon had found on the dresser.

"You know what it is, boyo. Have we not been hearing it since Master Enrico wrote he was coming across the sea? His train arrives at noon tomorrow and the missus isn't happy with the way the house looks. You and your brothers never cared what a house looked like, that's certain sure. It's clean, but it'll never be as fancy as what he's used to. Palaces, they are, the schools he goes to in Switzerland, or so I've heard. Well, don't just stand there. Where's the girleen?"

"I'm calling her Miss Morgan." He stepped out of the way, as Molly brushed past, "but I reckon when she gets to know us better she'll let us call her Elizabeth."

"Maybe we'll call her Miss Hoity-toity," Molly said moving along the corridor at the speed of a freight train.

"You have to go easy with a filly like that," Aldon hoped his aunt, who prided herself on saying exactly what she thought, would be courteous to the tired young woman downstairs.

"Aldon, you must begin as you mean to go on. You can't be too chummy with the help or they take advantage of you." Her words flowed back as her lace-up shoes hit the bottom stair and she strode toward the kitchen. "Come on, let's meet this filly." She settled into a sedate walk, patting her crown-braid as he paused at the door. Aldon reached around her to swing it open and she walked through as if she were queen of the kitchen, which come to think of it, she was. "Well, I never," she said, stopping abruptly and staring at the table.

There was Miss Morgan with her head down on her arms snoring gently. Aldon stared in wonder. He never knew ladies could snore.

"Ha," Molly poked the slender back and Miss Morgan jumped to her feet.

"I'm ready," Miss Morgan said, her eyes wild. Did she think she was somewhere else, he wondered.

"I got some stew on the stove," Molly spoke loudly as if to a simpleton. "Get plates and spoons and help yourselves."

Aldon went to get stew for both of them leaving Miss Morgan to figure out where she was and what was going on. "I wonder if you would consider going to church with us tomorrow," he said, trying to help her get oriented. He dipped a mug into the stew and filled the bowls. Miss Morgan sat down again, still groggy.

"I guess…" she hesitated.

"You can go to the Community Church with Aldon or the Catholic Church with Mr. Solano and me," Molly sat down across from her. She peered over the tops of her glasses.

"My mother tells me I was born in a convent home," Miss Morgan said. "So does that mean I'm Catholic? She shook her head. "No, maybe not." She looked at Molly frowning. "My grandparents are Scottish Presbyterian." She closed her eyes and laid her head on the top rung of the chair.

"You don't have to go to church," Aldon said concerned now about her exhaustion. "You might want to sleep in."

"No, no, I'll be fine," Miss Morgan lifting her head. "I'd like to know what God wants from me, if anything."

"The car will be ready to go at seven in the morning. Molly attends early mass and I practice with my pastor before the service begins." He looked at Molly, "You want her in my old room?"

"Yes, but first take her to the Solano's rooms, knock on the door, and introduce her, but watch out the missus doesn't get to talking. She's as lonely as a stray dog." Molly got the dishrag and wiped the table, which they had left as clean as when they started eating.

Upstairs, Miss Morgan slowed to look at the framed paintings on both sides of the hallway. Aldon waited remembering that when the Solanos moved in last year, the Signora ordered a tool with which to cut mats and he framed her pictures in hand-made pine frames. She painted in a frenzy, but he kept up with the demand because he made it his after-supper job in the evenings. Now that it was spring again and they were preparing to push the cattle into the mountains, Lia – Signora would have to stockpile her artworks or frame them herself until the push was over.

The boss's wife had asked him to pose for her, but he knew he never would unless it was out-of-doors, and Chief was in the picture. He had to admit she was an excellent painter, and he wouldn't mind having a portrait of his fine Appaloosa, especially if he could afford to buy it. When he tapped on the door, the woman opened it wearing a black, satin kimono with a big red poppy on it and her hair tumbling, shiny as obsidian, to her waist. Aldon looked away and introduced Miss Morgan without glancing at the Signora again.

CHAPTER 5

ALDON

"Oh, si, my new compagna." Lia stepped into the hallway and embraced Miss Morgan saying, "Welcome, we will have wonderful time together." Aldon had learned that compagna meant companion, so apparently Signora had big plans for using the newly hired Chicagoan. Molly, however, meant to use her for a kitchen maid. In all this scrambling, Aldon hoped there would be time for him to teach her to ride.

"Giovanni is asleeping in his room, but won't you come in?" The Signora was always hungry for company. Aldon couldn't blame her; the ranch was a good piece from town. But Aldon was concerned about the city gal's need for rest.

"Come on, we gotta get movin'." He tugged on her elbow, but she jerked her arm away and gave him an angry look. Even so, she went along the corridor with him.

"Home sweet home," He flung open the door to the room he'd slept in most of his life. The plank floor was clean, and the dresser that his grandfather had fashioned from cherry wood, glowed with polish. His old quilt lay across the foot of the bed. He now preferred to sleep under the thick, woolen army blanket he'd been allowed to bring home after his service in the Great War.

"If you keep going in the same direction we were headed, you'll come to the lavatory," he told her standing aside so she could enter the room.

"Thank you for everything." Miss Morgan's voice was cool and distant. He wondered what kind of a savage he appeared to her, manhandling her as he just had. He vowed to do better from here on out.

"If you can wait a few minutes, I'll fetch your trunk." He left then but sensed her slipping from the room and down the hall to the new bathroom with its long, German-made bathtub and flush toilet. Mr. Solano wanted things done right for his bride.

When he returned with the trunk, Miss Morgan lay across the bed fully dressed, but now sound asleep. She didn't stir when he removed her boots, rotated her by her feet until her head was on the pillow, and covered her with the quilt.

In the barn, he added air to the tires and put the oil and water back in. After filtering the gasoline, he funneled it into the tank. Tomorrow would be the automobile's first time out since the first snow-fall, and he was looking forward to getting behind the wheel. Mechanical things always worked for him. But he didn't know much about females. Ma fed the boys, kept them clean, and tried to make gentlemen of them, and one of the things she insisted upon was that they knew how to treat a lady. Another was that they never kept company with any other kind of woman. She told them what to look out for so that they didn't fall into a lifetime of having their hearts broken.

He grabbed the clean clothes Molly had laid out for him in the barn, picked up his towel and soap, and headed for the lake in the light of the stars and the crescent moon. The lake was one-of-a-kind as far as he knew. Of course, he hadn't seen every lake in the world, but this one had a hot spring at one end, and a place where the cold creek entered by waterfall at the other. In winter, they plunged into the warm water to bathe and in summer; they cooled off in the cold. What he liked was that both had shallow parts and deep parts. What he didn't like was the place in the middle where the water stayed tepid. He'd take hot or cold any day, but not the wishy-washy stuff in between.

He got out, dried off, and dressed, appreciating the clean clothes. Molly had laid out for him. He mentally thanked his mother, Nancy, who had trained him to wear clean clothes. Not all cowboys did. He wished Nancy would come on home where she belonged. He didn't get why she thought her sister Gertrude needed her more that he and Molly did. She's the best mother anyone ever had, he thought. She helped us stay morally clean by having us read the Bible to her every night before bed. She talked things over with us so that we understood how to work, how to save our money, and how to get along with other people. Dad taught us all about ranching. He never spared the rod where it might be needed, and I'm thankful for that, too.

He lay down on the cot in the loft alcove and pulled the heavy army blanket up to his chest. As soon as he let his body relax, his mind got to work again. He was back in his BeBe flying over France and into Germany not knowing whether he would die or return home a cripple. He rolled over and deliberately turned his mind to the young woman he'd just met. I hope she and I will be good friends, he thought. I'll see her again tomorrow. And maybe sometimes we can talk. I'll plant more wildflowers in the garden, she'll probably like those. He had many good things to think about: the songs he'd play on his mandolin tomorrow at church, the young woman, and driving the Flivver to church tomorrow.

CHAPTER 6

ELLIE

"Top o' the mornin' to you." The bed jiggled bringing Ellie out of a numbness of sleep. "Didn't you hear Mister Cock-o-the-Walk this mornin'?" She recognized Molly's voice. It rang with heartiness and good cheer and it annoyed Ellie beyond measure.

"I didn't hear anything," Ellie shaded her eyes with her hand as sunlight streamed in through the lace curtains. "What time is it?" she asked.

"Seven o'clock. I thought you might be wanting a bit of time to get ready and to have some rhubarb pie, fresh baked this mornin'. The milking is done. The chickens are fed. The sow is nursing her squealers. The garden is watered. Aldon has the Ford ready to go and Mr. Solano will be waiting in the front seat in one hour. The missus doesn't go to church. She's a heathern and still in bed as far as I can tell." Molly turned around and left the room forgetting to close the door behind her.

"Okay," Ellie sank back into the pillow to think. We're going to church. Signor Solano goes, but the signora stays home. Aldon is driving. I don't want any breakfast; maybe I'll snooze for one more minute.

"Come on, girleen, let's get going," Molly was back. She pulled off the covers and when Ellie opened her eyes, she realized that she was still in her clothes, but her boots had been removed and she'd been covered with a quilt. That said good things about Aldon. He was, apparently a gentleman.

"No rest for the wicked," Ellie said, hearing her grandmother admonishing her to rise and get to work. She sat up and looked around the room. Ah, her trunk. How thoughtful. Maybe the cowboy would turn out all right after all.

The trunk sat on its end, so all she had to do was open it as if it were a giant book. It had hangers and drawers and would have been worthy of a trip on the Queen Mary. Grandmother had succeeded in sending her off in high style, but suddenly the clothes she brought didn't seem appropriate for the setting she'd be living in. The traveling suit would be dressier and warmer, but she had slept in it for several nights and it wasn't what Grandmother would call, "fresh," anymore. The blue jersey would have to do, even though she wasn't fond of the long waists on dresses these days. She'd be glad when the styles changed again and she could buy a completely new wardrobe. On the other hand, now that she insisted on becoming independent, she wondered whether she'd ever have enough money to indulge her passion for clothes. *I hope Grandmother stops my allowance as I asked,* thought Ellie. I must prove to both of us that I am capable of taking care of myself.

She took out knickers and a crepe de chine envelope. She hoped no one would notice she was not wearing a corset. The corsetiere at the store had fitted her before she became an ambulance driver, but she couldn't be bound up when she had to move around freely and lift one end of the litters. She gloried in being able to get in and out of automobiles and bend over when necessary, but most of all, she had developed a fondness for breathing. People still gossiped about girls who were free in their dress and behavior, calling them flappers, Modern Millie's, or vamps. Ellie realized she must be careful not to fall into that category here where modern may have come for some things, but not all. She ran a brush through her hair but the air was so dry and full of electricity that it rose like a halo around her head. Grabbing her blue cloche she pulled it down to tame the strands that seemed to have a life of their own. She was glad ladies wore hats to church.

"What can I do to help," she asked Molly in the kitchen.

"Sit down and eat." Molly placed a piece of pie and a cup of cold milk on the table before her as she Ellie did what she asked. *Ordinarily I would consider the red juice against the white plate artful, but right now it reminds me of gallons of blood pouring from hundreds of screaming bodies.*

"I saw Aldon carry your violin case up last night," Molly said. "Or is that where you keep your eyebrows?"

"What?" It was too early for riddles. "No, my violin." Ellie brought out her salesgirl smile, and then realized Molly was referring to her thin eyebrows. She knew they weren't as thin as they could be, but she also knew that older women often disliked the new ways as much as younger people disdained the old ones.

"If God wanted us to have thin eyebrows, he would have drawn them on like I hear the floozies do."

"Yes, ma'am. I can let them grow if you want," said Ellie. She was on her way to independence. She was determined not to risk offending anyone and giving them an excuse to fire her.

"Eat your breakfast." Molly frowned. "We need to get going."

Ellie took up the fork and tasted the pie. It was so tart it made her ears ring. She grabbed the milk and gulped it down.

"I put six cups of sugar in that pie, my girl," Molly said. "Eat it up, now. We've waited a long winter for this rhubarb. Have you had your spring tonic yet?

"No, ma'am, but I'm sorry I can't eat it." Ellie stammered. "I'm just not hungry." She crossed her fingers hoping not to suffer repercussions for trying not to hurt Molly's feelin's.

"You liked the milk though?"

"Yes, it was good." Ellie nodded and kept on nodding until she realized she must resemble a bobble head doll.

"That there milk is from our own Brunhilda," Molly said with a smile. "It's got a lot of cream in it."

"I can tell!" Ellie confirmed. "It's good and cold, too."

"Aldon will teach you how to milk Brunhilda. It can be part of your kitchen duties. Besides, everybody ought to know how to milk a cow.

Well, now, if you're not going to eat that pie, scrape it into the bucket under the sink, and we'll give it to the pig, she's eating for thirteen. I gotta admit, even with all that sugar, it's still a mite tart." She walked out laughing to herself and Ellie knew everything was all right for the time being.

CHAPTER 7

ELLIE

"How do, Miss Morgan." Mr. Leitzinger stood at attention near the driver's side of the Flivver. "Ready for church?"

She nodded looking him over and noting the way his Stetson enhanced the western theme of his jacket and boots. The jacket was as handsomely tailored as any tuxedo she'd seen and his boots had been carefully polished. He must have a place for clothes in the house, she thought. Surely he doesn't keep them in the barn loft.

"Mr. Leitzinger, I've decided you may call me Ellie," She looked into blue-gray eyes shaded by thick, perfectly shaped, brows.

"Good! Call me Aldon, please. Will you step around to the other side and meet Signor Solano?" Aldon steered her to the white-haired gentleman in the passenger seat. The man wore a perfectly cut, pinstriped suit and held a black fedora on his lap. She was surprised at the sartorial wonders in this place. She placed her hand on the windowsill and the older man lifted it to his lips. A diamond cufflink on his shirtsleeve peeked out, caught a sunbeam, and winked its brilliance.

"Good Morning, Signorina. You are welcome to Spruce Creek Ranch. Please make yourself at home with us. Today, you are our guest to church."

"Thank you, sir, she said, carefully slipping the hand he had kissed into the pocket of her spring jacket.

"Now will you come over here, please?" Aldon, again at the driver's side pulled the seat forward so she could get into the back with Molly who sat behind Signor Solano. The older woman wore a heavy black coat russet streaked with age. The hat she wore came from the start of the century and sprouted stiff lavender ribbons looping and turning in a fantasy of bows. Ellie couldn't help but admire its vintage elegance.

Aldon got behind the wheel, pressed on the starter, and the automobile hummed to life. They were on their way to town, an older man, a woman of a certain age, and two young people who still had most of their lives ahead of them.

It took fifteen minute and a few seconds to coast down Main Street. On the other side two identical churches faced each other across the road.

"This is the Catholic Church." Aldon wheeled in next to the north-facing edifice, got out and opened the door for Signor Solano and held the seat back for Molly. A priest in a cassock rushed from the church, gave Signor Solano a hug, and kissed his cheeks. Ellie noticed that Aldon's face turned red and assumed he was embarrassed. She knew men in Chicago disdained a show of affection, so she wasn't surprised that cowboys did too.

"That's Father Contenti," Aldon said. "We'll leave the car here and walk across to my church. Opening the luggage area, he picked up a large, black Bible and stuck it under his arm then lifted his mandolin case and closed the trunk.

A large young man in a dark blue suit, red hair flaming in the sun, met them. He pumped Aldon's hand and hit him on the shoulder. *Ah, that's how the men greet each other here,* thought Ellie.

"Hello there, I'm Pastor Quentin Rudd of the Clifton Community Church, at your service ma'am." He gave a small bow then led Ellie into the church and straight to a pot-bellied stove which radiated heat. "It's still chilly out in the morning. Come get warm," he said. She held her gloved hands above the heat rising from the stove. Looking around she all but gasped at the sight of jeweled light shining through the stained glass windows, dashing color against the white walls, and splashing over the tops of the pews.

"You have a musician's hands, I think," Pastor Rudd said.

"Thank you, I play the violin." She looked around the large room.

"Your church is lovely." One of the windows depicted Jesus leading a herd of sheep with a lamb lying contently across his shoulders; another showed Him kneeling against a rock with His hands folded in prayer. Light surrounded him.

"The first one is an artist's rendering of the Good Shepherd," said Pastor Rudd following her gaze. "The second is our Savior's prayer in the Garden of Gethsemane not long before His Crucifixion and Atonement."

By this time, Aldon had seated himself in a wooden chair at the front and was concentrating on tuning his mandolin.

Pastor Rudd walked with Ellie to a front pew and motioned for her to be seated. He then went over to an organ that looked too small for him and fitted himself onto the bench. Angling his feet so he could press the pedals he laid large fingers on the keys. He and Aldon struck up "A Mighty Fortress is our God." Ellie had heard it before at Grandmother's church, but never like this. Her heart rose up and she felt as if she could fly to heaven on the music alone.

When the men finished playing, Pastor Rudd disappeared through a door at the side of the church. Ellie gave Aldon a look that asked where he was going. "Young'uns outdoor Sunday School," he said catching the look. He beckoned to the ladies who were coming in at the back and hanging their coats on a coat tree to come forward.

"Please come closer," he said. The women wore print housedresses and ancient hats. When Ellie looked at their feet she saw white anklets with stout lace-up shoes. Looking up to scan the women's faces, she saw eyes bright with anticipation. *What kind of lives must they lead?* It's probably a constant round of child-care, cooking, washing dishes, cleaning and sewing. What could they do for entertainment except come to town for church on Sunday? *Could I bear every day being like the one before it and the one after? Oh well, I suppose happiness depends more on attitude than anything else.* Aldon introduced her to Mrs. Bauer, Mrs. McGregor, and a Leitzinger cousin named Natty.

"How do you do?" Ellie said the words she'd been taught to say when she met someone. The ladies nodded without smiling, and suddenly Ellie knew she was being judged. Oh Lord, she thought they'll be gossiping about me the minute I leave the church.

Let's pray," Aldon bowed his head, and the women bowed theirs, too. "Lord, please open our ears, eyes, and hearts and help us know you in fresh, new ways."

"Ellie," Aldon said, smiling. "Will you please read Psalm 139:14?" He opened his Bible and pointing to the passage, put it into her hands.

"I will praise thee; for I am fearfully and wonderfully made: marvelous are thy works; and that my soul knoweth right well." Ellie projected as she had been taught in drama class." Was it true? Was she fearfully and wonderfully made? What a fine thought that was. She paused to let it sink in, and a momentary hush fell over the company as if her own awe had become a benediction for them all. Then, in a gentle voice, Aldon assigned a scripture to Mrs. McGregor and she began to read.

CHAPTER 8

ELLIE

When the service was over, Pastor Rudd stood at the door of the church shaking hands with the departing church members. Ellie and Aldon came last because people wanted to talk to Aldon. Ellie waited beside him and came to know the respect the community had for him.

When they walked to the door and stopped before the preacher Aldon invited him to the Fitzgerald's for coffee. "We have something to discuss as a community." Aldon said.

"Ellie, you come along, you'll be involved, too."

"Hold up a minute, Aldon. I have a question for this young lady." The pastor turned to Ellie. "Would you consider taking our children's Sunday School class, Miss Ellie?"

"I don't know much about the Bible or teaching children," she stammered.

"Well, please pray about it. We can give you materials to study and it would be a big help. I'm teaching the little darlings right now but, if you were willing to do it, I could use the time to pray and polish my sermon."

"I guess I could think about it." Ellie answered. She couldn't understand why he'd ask her when there were many others more capable.

"And would you think about playing your violin with Aldon and me for the beginning of the service? We practice on Wednesday nights before prayer meeting."

She didn't see how she could do all with the jobs she had at the ranch, but she'd talk to Aldon about it. She did want to help and be accepted into the community.

The Fitzgerald's parlor was spacious and comfortable. It held a mix of old and new furniture, which included enough chairs for everyone. Kenny and his mother served the coffee in china cups and set out plates of pastry. Signor Solano and Father Contenti, who had changed out of his vestments, sat on either side of the inactive fireplace. Ellie, Molly, Aldon, and Pastor Rudd arrayed themselves around the room. Mr. and Mrs. Fitzgerald sat together on a Victorian couch. After helping his mother serve, Kenny disappeared.

Aldon made introductions. The priest stood and smiled at Ellie. She didn't know whether to bow or shake hands, but Aldon moved her on as Father Contenti sat down again. The priest folded his hands waiting for the din of conversation to fade. His snow-white hair lifted in a breeze from an open window. As he began to speak, Signor Solano nodded his head in affirmation obviously knowing what was coming.

"I have called you together to ask for your help. You heard about the Negro man who worked at the saloon?" The priest looked at Aldon.

"Yes, Sir. He always manned the chuck wagon for cattle drives and round-ups, called it his vacation." The room fell silent for a moment.

"Did you know he sent for his wife?" Mrs. Fitzgerald asked. Aldon nodded, a serious expression in his eyes. "She arrived with a small child on Friday – their granddaughter. She has no job and they have no home. We're wondering if you might look after the two of them at the ranch for a while." Father Contenti glanced at Molly.

"Is she a good worker?" Molly asked. "With so many coming to stay at the house, I'm going to need more help." Molly crossed her legs at the ankles and leaned back.

"She has helped me a good bit since she's been here. In fact, she made the pastries." Mrs. Fitzgerald picked up the plate of baked goods and passed it to Mr. Fitzgerald who made everyone laugh by lifting his pinkie finger as he made a show of choosing the perfect treat. "She's a fine cook, but the child is quite young and needs someone to look after her every minute. We just can't manage the time."

"No, Mrs. Fitzgerald, you cannot." Father Contenti spoke in a firm voice. "You have too much work already for the three of you: the general store, the livery, the movie theater, and me. Mrs. Fisher …"

"She asks that we call her Kate," said Mrs. Fitzgerald breaking in. "She doesn't talk much, but I did learn that she and her husband saved for her fare and a cabin here. I don't know what happened to the savings. The child's name is Seraphina. Her mother and father are in prison back East for robbing banks."

"At first we thought Kate might relieve the Fitzgeralds of looking after the parish house and me, but there's one thing we need to consider," said Father Contenti.

"The clan," Aldon said knowingly. "They'll be on the look-out for Kate and Seraphina, especially since the two of them passed through Denver, Artesia, and Clifton. The clan seems to know everything these days."

"Yes." Father Contenti agreed.

"They aren't primarily after people of color, here, though as they seem to be in the South." said Mrs. Fitzgerald.

"No," said Aldon. "They're after Jewish people and Catholics, and anyone from a foreign country, even England. They're afraid a group will start taking jobs and turning around to get their relatives hired and that way take over our community. They haven't hurt anyone too badly, yet. I don't think, however, that they'd hesitate to come after someone like Kate, do you?"

We will be happy to take them," said Signor entering the conversation. "Perhaps Miss Morgan could help look after the bambina?"

"Of course, Signor," Ellie said. "I am in your employ. I am not familiar with children, but I will do my best."

"Signora Solano, my dear wife, will be delighted to help. It is what she needs to fill her life." Signor Solano lifted his head listening as a train whistle sounded over the valley."

"Your grandson has arrived." Standing, Aldon pulled his gold watch from his pocket and glanced at it. "Right on time. Shall we go meet him? Molly, will you and Mrs. Fitz help the woman get ready for the ranch? Ellie is coming with us to the station." He lifted an eyebrow in Ellie's direction and she nodded *yes*. "Quentin, can we prevail upon you to bring a load of people to the ranch in your Bearcat? Molly will give you a sandwich for your trouble."

Five minutes later, Aldon, Ellie, and Signor Solano got out of the Ford and hurried to the boardwalk to watch for Signor's grandson. When Ellie spotted a young man in a suit and fedora with an umbrella on his arm, she knew it was Enrico. With soft, dark curls resting on the collar of his jacket, he resembled a poet from the Romance period. The Signor sagged momentarily against Ellie, so she slipped her arm around his thin waist to support him. He soon straightened his shoulders and stood tall, waiting to greet a boy who had become a man. Enrico paused to set his Panama at a jaunty angle. When he looked up and saw his grandfather, his face lit with the smile of an angel. Aldon retrieved Enrico's small case and paid the porter who had been carrying it.

Signor Solano threw his arms around Enrico. When they both began to cry he took a handkerchief from his pocket and dabbed first at Enrico's tears and then his own.

"Name's Aldon Leitzinger," Aldon said, moving to shake hands.

Ellie would learn in the weeks to come that Enrico's entire family had been scattered at the beginning of the war. Signor Solano had decided to leave him in boarding school in Switzerland so he could finish the excellent education he was getting there. When peace came, his parents were dead and he wanted to come to America, but his grandfather said he must finish at university. He had a degree in music now and was ready to move into the next phase of his life.

After putting Enrico's suitcase in the car, the two men got into the back seat because they wanted to sit together. Ellie got into the passenger seat, and when she glanced back, she saw that grandfather and grandson were holding each other's hands as if they would never let go. She was so happy to see Signor Solano receiving the gift of a precious family member.

CHAPTER 9

ELLIE

Aldon parked the Ford next to the barn and Pastor Rudd pulled his Stutz up behind it. Ellie got out and followed Molly, Kate, and Seraphina up to the house. She paused at the back steps and looked back to see what the men were doing.

Aldon, the Signor, and Enrico stood next to Pastor Rudd, who had lifted the hood of his car, and seemed to be explaining its workings. Ellie found, however, that Enrico was watching her. She turned away confused. Had she done or said something to make him think she wanted his attention? She recalled only that one thought at the train station about how good-looking he was. Had it shown on her face?

By the time she got to her room, changed into a cotton dress, and descended to the kitchen, Molly was bustling around like a waitress in a train station cafe.

"Oh here she is at last," Molly said. "Ellie, Signor Solano believes in a Sabbath Day of rest for servants as well as for the master, so we're having sandwiches for our noon meal." Before Ellie could reply, Molly spoke to Kate, who stood with her back to the counter and the child half covered with her shawl leaning against her.

Because Kate wore a calico head-rag that hid any grayness in her hair, and because she had a young-looking face, it was hard to think of her as grandmother to four or five year old. Kate's long-fingered hands rested lightly on the child's chest, probably to keep her out of the way until Molly told what to do.

"Are you hungry?" Molly inquired of the girl.

"Yes," Seraphina nodded without looking up.

"Yes, ma'am," Kate tapped her finger on the girl's collar bone before speaking to Molly. "She fine, Miss."

"I'll say who is fine in me own kitchen if you please." Molly's mouth pursed. "Sure'n it's my house to run. If somebody is hungry here, they will eat, or I'll know the reason why."

"Yes'm," Kate said. She had a wary look that told Ellie she wasn't one to talk back.

"Butter a piece of bread for the child and sprinkle plenty of sugar on it," Molly told Ellie.

"Does Seraphina, mean angel?" Molly asked. Kate nodded without speaking and Molly went on. "She might have some Caucasian, as well as Indian in her. I don't know what tribes you have where you come from but here we have the Utes, mostly they're all gone now, though."

Ellie had found the bread on the counter, sliced off a piece, slathered it with butter, and then sprinkled sugar over it. The child looked up with an impish grin as she handed it to her.

"Ah, she'll be something when she grows up," said Molly. "You can tell from those light hazel eyes that she's a smart one. Here in our valley, everyone gets along. Folks help each other. During the Great War, we people with ancestors from Germany, England, and Ireland buried our young men in the community cemetery and mourned our losses together. Ellie, get the ham out of the refrigerator. We traded five pounds of beef for that. It's a treat to have something different for a change." Molly seemed to be letting off steam by talking whether anyone was listening or not. "Kate sit that child down at the table and make yourself useful. You and Ellie can make the sandwiches on that counter over there, assembly line style like that Mr. Ford up there in Michigan."

"Kate I knew your husband," Molly said slicing radishes into a bowl of lettuce from the ranch garden. Next, she added sliced carrots and scallions. "Cookie, we called him. He was a good humble man. I'll bet you were surprised when you got here and found out he was gone. I knew him from working to prepare food for cattle drives. Once

Aldon's Ma moved to Artesia, we needed a camp cook and he applied, even though he worked most of the time at the saloon. He probably had a real good reason for what he did to that gambler fella."

Ellie, for one, was listening closely; she wanted to know about the community she had moved into. What had Mr. Fisher done? Why did he make a serious mistake right when his wife and granddaughter were on their way to join him?

"Kate and Seraphina can sleep in the room next to yours, Ellie. The child must be with her granny so she won't be scared. The rooms are already clean because I regularly mop the floors and risk my life washing those windows by sitting on the sill with the top of me hanging outside. I need to train both of you and that will take me all my time. But you'll do for help and company until Aldon's mother, Nancy, gets tired of working in the café with her sister and comes back to us."

Just then, Signora Solano came into the kitchen. She wore a red silk dress with jet beads swinging from a generous bosom. The beads were no blacker or shinier than her hair, which she wore, in a low bun on the nape of her neck. To Ellie, it looked ready to fall down at any minute. She wore high-heeled shoes but had a cloth wrapped around her ankle as if she'd been hurt.

"What happened to your leg?" Molly asked.

"It is no business of yours," said the Signora lifting her chin. "I am the mistress here, not you." Then suddenly she noticed the child and squatted down next to her at the table.

"Bella, bella! Who are you, bambina?"

"I am Seraphina and I am five-years-old." The child showed five fingers. "I want to be four, but Granny says I already been that and I can't go back to be it again. How old are you?"

Kate stepped over, rapped Seraphina lightly on the head, and hissed. With pouty mouth, the child looked up at her from under scowling eyebrows.

"I'm four times five," Signora Solano answered ignoring the older woman. "Do you know how old that is? Have you learned to cipher, yet?"

"What's cipher?" the child demanded letting a smile come out.

"Adding, subtracting. It's arithmetic." Signora reached up and cupped the girl's chin in her hand, but Seraphina jerked her head away.

"We don't teach arithmetic to such young children around here," Molly broke in. "They can't learn it."

"Do you like stories, little one?" Signora spoke directly to the child.

"Oh, yes. I will give you my sugar bread if you will tell me a story." She offered the crust, which was all she had left.

"You behave now, chile. This lady ain't got time for the likes of you," Kate spoke sternly. "Pardon, ma'am, but our last lady took time with her and now the chile she think she somethin'"

Ignoring the grandmotherly tirade, Signora Solano rose and saw Ellie. "Your hair! I did not notice it when we met last night."

"What's wrong with it?" Ellie's hands flew to her head.

"It's bobbed!" Signora Solano sang out.

"Yes, ma'am." Ellie nodded. "But I can grow it, if you …"

"No, no, I want mine bobbed, too." Signora Solano automatically started pushing in hairpins that had come loose from the chignon on the back of her neck. "It is heavy, it falls down, it is hot."

"Oh, yes, ma'am, perhaps you would allow me to style it for you." Ellie took a deep breath.

Seraphina put her hands in her hair and pulled straight up. "My hair is heavy, it falls down, it is hot," she whined

CHAPTER 10

ALDON

After putting the ranch to bed, Aldon arrived at his loft sanctuary and stretched on the cot in a state of annoyance. Sunday was the one day in the week when he let up on the ranch work. Half the afternoon, though, he had sat at the table listening to what was called *conversation*. The other half the afternoon had passed showing Enrico the ranch. The man wanted to know how to run it and the worth of it. You'd have thought Signor's grandson planned to inherit it.

Too bad we couldn't have started Ellie's riding lessons today, he thought. *Oh, well, no use crying over spilt milk. As Ma says, it has enough water in it already.*

He picked up the Bible from his bedside table and opened it to the Psalms. Lately, he had come to believe that the Master spoke to him whenever he read David's words.

Soon he laid down the Bible, checked the level of kerosene in the lamp, and propped his back against the wall. Holding a lined tablet on his drawn up knees he started writing to his surviving brother.

Dear Bill,

    It's Sunday and the chores are done. I'm sleeping in the loft these days because the house is filling up with people. I sleep fine until the new cockerel starts in. Mother named him Chanticleer the Twenty-Fifth. He practices crowing anytime of the night or day. Howling coyotes set him off and at three-thirty in the morning, he has to notify us that the train is arriving in the valley. He must think the headlight is the sun.

How are you doing in Hollywoodland? We would like to see you. Don't see much of Ma, either.

Pastor Rudd has been encouraging us to read the Bible. I think it's helping me get over the war some. I lost some friends, but we fly-boys didn't suffer like the men in the trenches did.

I'm beginning to believe that praying is going to help us know what to do about the possibility of losing the ranch. I sure would hate to see that happen after our dad and granddad kept it going so long, with us in mind. Right now, I can't see how we'd get along without Signor Solano's lease money, but sometimes he talks about going back to Italy. If he does that before we get a plan, we're sunk.

The Appaloosa is fine, thanks for asking. I named him Chief. He's got all the colors, white, russet, black, and some sorrel. He's a beauty of a mustang. There's a few more up there I'm interested in, too. They are wild and they belong to anybody who can catch them. The winters are hard on them and we can give them a good home or maybe sell some to the ranchers here about. Come on home and help me bring them in

Remember I told you about the young woman who was coming to work here? I picked her up at the train station about suppertime yesterday. Her name is Miss Elizabeth Morgan. I'm thinking on asking her to take Cookie's place on the cattle drive. After all, she came west to have some adventures.

Write and tell me about your stunt job and the horses in your remuda. I'm glad you got away for a while. You don't have any broken bones yet, do you? I'm sure you're their best rider. I'd put you up against anyone when it comes to horses. Tell us when you star in a moving picture show and we'll go to town and see it.

Say, Bill, have you come across any of those flappers yet? The reason I ask is that I'm trying to figure out if Miss Morgan might be one. Mother always told us to stay away from women who bob their hair and wear lipstick and Miss Morgan does both. She's independent, too, like you hear about women being these days.

Miss Morgan says she's a mechanician. I call it mechanic but can hardly believe she knows anything about motors. I can tell that it makes her mad that I don't take her serious. I heard about those ambulance drivers and the women in America who did all kinds of driving during the war. That was fine, but I've never yet met a woman who could clean spark plugs, change oil, or patch tires, nor one who'd want to.

I'm going to teach her to shoot and fish. Do you think she ought to use the Sharpe's or the Remington? No question which fishing rod she'll use, yours, of course, if it's okay?

Oops. The barn cat leaped up to see what I was doing and rubbed her cheek on the end of my pencil. She can't stay long, as she has four kittens to feed, so I stopped to pet her for a bit. Her purr is so loud it sounds like a tractor starting up.

We brought a colored woman and her granddaughter home from town. She was Cookie Fisher's wife. You remember how he called our cattle drive his vacation? I don't feel like writing about what happened but I'll tell you later.

Write soon.
Best Regards, from
Your brother, Aldon

CHAPTER 11

ELLIE

The next morning, something woke Ellie before dawn, but she felt refreshed and eager to see what the day might bring. Pulling her print dress from the closet where she had hung it the night before, she picked up her work shoes and tiptoed down the stairs. Each time a wooden stair creaked, she stopped to listen to the sleeping house. She was sitting in a kitchen chair bending over and tying the laces on her shoes when Aldon walked in carrying a bouquet that looked small in his long-fingered hands.

"Whoa," he said pausing dramatically as if her presence in the kitchen had startled him. "You're up early." He stepped into the small room off the kitchen and came back with a blue teapot into which he ran water for the flowers.

"I don't know what woke me. Those are pretty," she said watching him settle the flowers into the water and put the pot on the table in front of her.

"A few wildflowers that grew out by the barn. Weeds, I guess, but yeah, they're kinda pretty." His hand hovered over the flowers in the teapot.

"Do you pick them often?" she asked.

"Nah, haven't done it since I was a kid. It felt like a good day for it, that's all." He glanced away.

41

"They are fine wildflowers," she said wanting him to know that she, appreciated them. "If you'll show me where everything is, I'll make coffee." She looked up at him and from that angle; he appeared to be seven feet tall.

"Well, let's get it going." He opened the stove lid and poked at the banked coals, then added kindling from the box on the floor. The embers flickered into flame, and the scent of wood-smoke perfumed the air reminding Ellie of trips to the Poconos with the Campfire Girls.

"Where do you keep the coffee?" Ellie asked, getting up and going to the stove. She grabbed the tin pot off the stove-shelf and filled it.

Aldon pulled a package from the cupboard and showed her the label. "How about Arbuckle's Arioso? Everybody around here likes it, except Signora Solano. She sticks with Italian coffee."

"Yes, we drink it in Chicago, too. Would you like for me to make an omelet?" Ellie looked into the lower cupboards and brought out a frying pan.

"Sounds good. I haven't had a real omelet since France."

"I learned how to make them from the chef in our restaurant at the department store. They were all the rage for brunch. The secret is to cook the eggs as slowly as possible," Ellie said. "Do you have any cheese?"

"Good German cheese – made by my uncle. It's in the pantry under a cloth." Aldon went to get the cheese and Ellie followed him, sightseeing. She noted that the room held staple foodstuffs, extra dishes, and large pots and pans.

"How is it you know so much about the kitchen?" she asked.

"Nancy, taught us boys to cook. She could run cattle, so she figured we needed to know about women's work in case no girls wanted to marry us when we grew up." Aldon grinned and started grating the cheese.

"Nancy is your mother, right? Why do you call her Nancy?" Ellie saw a bowl of eggs in the pantry, and took them into the kitchen to break into a bowl.

"We started calling her that to tease her and it stuck." He opened a drawer and pulled out a wooden spoon. "Will this work?" he asked.

He poured the coffee and set out cream and sugar while Ellie cooked the omelet and divided it onto two plates. "I'm finding out I have several bosses, and it's confusing," she said sitting down and admiring the view of the valley through the many-paned windows. He sat beside her, and she assumed it was so he could see the valley below, too.

"Your number one boss would be Signor Solano," Aldon instructed, but he said I could take you on the cattle drive if you have no objection. Next, it would be Molly, unless Signora wants you with her. Sounds like you'll be busy, but it will be all right. I'm here most of the time, so if you need help, let me know." He put a forkful of eggs in his mouth, chewed, and closed his eyes in ecstasy. "Mmm. You'll give Molly a run for her money."

"Don't say that. I don't want to offend her in any way." Ellie put her hand on his wrist, but removed it immediately when a spark of electricity shocked her.

"What do you think about the cattle drive?" he said, seemingly unaware of the effect touching him had on her.

"May I think about it?" Ellie took a deep breath to calm herself. She hadn't felt so alive in a long time.

"It's a small herd," he said, "The ranch families are all related to each other. We take a bunch of cattle into the range so they can graze through the summer. That allows the grass to grow, and then in the wintertime we use it for hay."

"Would I be riding a horse, though?" Her enthusiasm stalled like a bicycle going up a steep hill.

"Yep. Ribbons can make one more push. She knows the way. By the end of the first day, you'll feel as if you've been in a rocking chair."

"Ah, yes?" She was skeptical. "What will I do to earn my pay?"

"We need a new cook," Aldon said. "I've been to town looking for one, but there's no one around who can or will do it."

"Who did it last year?"

"Believe it or not, it was Kate's husband, Albert Fisher." Aldon's eyebrows came together in a frown. "We called him Cookie – that's what we call camp cooks."

"Doesn't he want to go?" she asked. From the agonized expression on Aldon's face, she wasn't sure she wanted to hear the answer.

"He was the first person to try out the new electric chair down at the state penitentiary." Aldon's voice wavered, and she could tell he felt sad, but he went on. "He was a good cook, and a decent man. I'm sorry he got into trouble."

"What did he do?" she asked.

"Well…he killed a man. I'll tell you about it sometime." Aldon got up for the coffee pot and sat back down again. "For now, do you want the job?"

"I don't have a lot of experience with cooking," she admitted. "My mother stayed at home and looked after the house and I spent most of my spare time with my grandparents at the store."

"You strike me as someone who could learn to do anything," he said. "If you did make a mistake or two, I doubt if the cousins would shoot you, they're partial to good-looking girls." He winked and bobbed his head.

"Shoot me! What do you mean?" Ellie sipped at the coffee left in the bottom of her mug, but she immediately started coughing and he began to pat her back. Once she caught her breath, she went on, "Why would anyone shoot a cook?"

"The men expect things to be just right, even though most of the time they're only getting coffee, beans, bacon, and biscuits. My grandpa liked to tell a story about a cook that made coffee as weak as Chinese tea and biscuits as hard as bullets. One of the fellows was in a bad mood, because he got kicked by a horse. He whipped out his sidearm and shot the cook dead. It has been a warning to cooks ever since. Don't worry, though, they wouldn't do that to you, even if you burned the beans."

Ellie assumed burning the beans was the worst thing a camp cook could do.

"So, do you want to ride along?" He seemed eager for her answer.

"You promise they won't shoot me?" She looked up at him with a half-smile to let him know she now understood that he was joking.

"I promise." He nodded. "Kenny's going too. You know that tall drink-a-water that belongs to the Fitzgeralds. He's a good boy and a hard worker, and he'll look after you."

"I'll need someone to look after me for sure," she said.

"We'll castrate and brand tomorrow, and then you and Molly can start getting the food ready. She's lived around here all her life, and she and Nancy went on many a drive. But she figures now it's her job to keep the home fires burning."

At the same moment, they looked into each other's eyes realizing he had mentioned the name of a song from the war. He started humming in a pure baritone. With a look, he asked her to join him. Their voices blended as if they'd been singing together all their lives.

"Keep the homes fires burning,

Though your hearts are yearning,

Though your lads are far away

They dream of home."

As they finished the song, she glanced up to see that someone was on the other side of the swinging door listening.

CHAPTER 12

ELLIE

Molly pushed open the door, let it swing shut behind her, and stood staring at Ellie and Aldon. "What's all that caterwauling about?" Molly put her hands on her hips and looked at Aldon, waiting for an answer.

"Well now, that's not caterwauling, Ma'am, that's singing, and mighty fine, too, I'd say." Aldon placed his hand over his heart.

"Go on with you, boyo. I'm ready to fix breakfast for the Solanos, so get out of my way." Molly nodded toward the back door.

"Can I help?" Ellie asked.

"Cut an orange in half, slice it, and cut it again so you'll have triangles the Signor can pick up with his fingers. Take it up to him while I get the rest of the breakfast. Be certain-sure he has a damp napkin to wipe his fingers on."

"Before I ride into town, I need to talk to you for a minute, Molly," said Aldon. He pulled out a chair and she sat down with a snort of impatience.

"Are you still here? What do you want? I've got to get me work started or I'll be behind all the day." Molly's strident voice carried easily to Ellie who stood at the counter cutting a large navel orange. "Young woman, I've had the oatmeal simmering all night. After you take the orange up, come back and get the rest of the breakfast for the Solanos, and take it up."

"Mr. Solano has given me permission to take Ellie on the cattle push." Aldon's voice was low and controlled.

"Over my dead body! I've got all the cooking, and then I'll be training Kate, and somebody has to look after the bairn, plus who knows what that Enrico might dream up. I still have Signor and Signorina, though I don't know why she can't help."

"Ellie will help with the shopping and cooking and once we've gone you'll have time to do everything you need to. The cousins and I, Ellie, and Kenny, will only be at the camp one night." Aldon's voice held respectful confidence.

"What do you have to say for yourself, young lady, now that you've wheedled your way into Aldon's favor?" Molly spoke over her shoulder to Ellie, who had finished cutting the big orange and started to leave the room.

The accusation short-circuited Ellie's thinking and she froze in the middle of the room with the plate in her hand.

"Molly," Aldon spoke in a tone of gentle reproof and Ellie was released to move on. She pushed the door open feeling like a coward but grateful to leave the cranky Molly in Aldon's hands.

When she knocked on the door of the suite upstairs, Signor Solano called out a melodious, "Entrare."

Shifting the plate of orange slices, she opened the door with her right hand. The Signor sat at his desk with the sun slanting in behind him, turning his white hair into a halo of silver, and reminding her of her grandfather. He made room for the plate amongst a pile of papers.

"Ah, the color of an orange! What a beautiful sight. Thank you, my dear." Tilting his head to look at her he smiled and started to rise, but she motioned for him to remain seated. "I regret that the Signora is still a-sleeping," he said. "She will be sorry she missed you."

Back in the kitchen, Ellie discovered that her singing partner had made his escape and that Kate and Seraphina stood against the counter as they had the day before, waiting for instructions. Molly began to oblige them by giving a lecture, so Ellie saw no choice but to pause and listen too.

"Aldon is meeting his cousins at the feedlot in town to help bring the cattle home. We keep them there over the worst of the winter, but we brand them here before they go up into the range for the summer to graze. This is the smallest herd we've ever had, only about five hundred, or so." She shook her head. "So many things have happened to the original bunch: drought, blizzards, starvation, and disease. In time, even these ones will be sold for beef and then they'll all be gone. I don't know what's to become of us after that. Signor Solano surely can't afford to keep pouring money into this place forever." She took Seraphina's hand and pulled her away from her grandmother who reluctantly let go.

"Take this little one upstairs, Ellie. Signora told me yesterday that she wants to look after her this mornin' while we cook the meal for the crew." Molly said. "Then come back and get the breakfast."

Ellie wondered whether Molly knew that the Signora was still in bed but decided not to stir the housekeeper's wrath. As she and Seraphina climbed the stairway, the child asked one question after another in such rapid succession that there were no quiet spaces to insert an answer.

"Where are we going? When will we eat? Do I have to eat oatmeal?" Ellie was delighted with the child's curiosity and the way she expressed herself. She looked forward to befriending and perhaps teaching Seraphina a few useful things.

"Ah, the little one." Signor had finished his orange slices and handed Ellie the empty plate and napkin. "Come here," he said in a soft voice. When the child did as he said, he bent over in his chair and looked into her face while she looked back with equal interest. "I will give her a pencil and paper and she will draw for me here on the floor," he said. "Signora will rise soon.

When Ellie got back to the kitchen, Molly told her Kate was doing laundry out in the yard. "There you are. It took you long enough. It's six o'clock already and the cow hasn't been milked, nor have the chickens been fed. I'll show you where things are." She opened a drawer in the cabinet under the counter. "Tea towels in the top drawer, clean dust rags in the bottom one.

"I've soaked the beans, so we can start the noon meal, and then we'll go to the barn. Ellie, you put them on the stove to boil for chili, then fry up some of that beef in the butcher paper, over there. They ground it at the general store in town, where we keep our own freezer-locker. When the men go hunting, we take the venison and elk to town, too. We used to do the meat-cutting ourselves. Modern times are better."

As soon as the chili bubbled on the back of the stove, Ellie received instruction in the arts of milking a cow, feeding chickens, and gathering eggs. About the time they finished they heard cows mooing and the, "*yips*" and "*hies*" of the men driving them. Laundry on the line, Kate joined them as they stepped out to watch Aldon and several other men on horses driving the cattle into a field next to the corral and separating some out to take into the closed space.

CHAPTER 13

ELLIE

Molly stepped onto the bottom log of the enclosure and put her arms over the top one to balance herself. Ellie, taking her lead, helped Kate up, and the three women waited for the action to begin. Ellie saw the handles of the branding irons sticking out of the fire in the middle of the enclosure.

"It won't be long now," Molly shouted. She waved to one of the older cowboys. "There's Jim, he married my cousin."

"Good morning." Aldon rode over on one of the most beautiful horses Ellie had ever seen. Its white mane and tail blew free and the colors on its hide reminded her of a brown, black, and burnt orange painting she'd seen on a white background at a gallery.

"Is that Chief?" Ellie asked, remembering her few conversations with Aldon. The horse nodded its head tack jangling as if giving an answer, but Ellie suspected it was only impatient.

"Yeah, he's an Appaloosa." Aldon answered.

"I like his hair," she hid a smile, knowing her choice of words would tease Aldon. He hesitated before speaking, but then he smiled too.

"Most of his breed has one or two colors, but he got all four." Aldon touched the brim of his Stetson. "We'll get to work, now, kid. So long." He gave the animal a light kick with the heel of his boot and they were away.

Ellie, watched as Aldon threw a rope under a calf's hoof, catching him in a loop. The rope taut, Aldon gave Chief a signal to Chief pull the calf to the fire. Molly's cousin's husband threw the calf to the ground and tied its feet together.

The creature bellowed as another man shoved a red-hot iron into its hip. Sizzle and smoke from the burning brand, and the odor of singed hair reminded Ellie back of the day the permanent wave machine malfunctioned and singed the curls on a patron's head. The smell, combined with the memory made feel her sick, so she lowered her head hoping she wouldn't embarrass herself. She didn't think anyone saw her distress, but when she looked up, Molly scowled at her.

Trying to distract herself, Ellie looked into the center of the pen where the young bovine had been released to return to its mother. A cowboy, down on one knee tossed something white that looked like baby eggplants into a galvanized bucket.

"There now," said Molly, "that's the castration done. Those Rocky Mountain oysters in the bucket are a treat for the men. They insist on frying those theirselves. They think a woman can't do it, but I was frying them when they were only gleams in their daddy's eyes, so they needn't tell me there's anything a woman can't do. We have to finish dinner, and then start on supper." Molly stepped down and started back toward the house. The other two followed.

"Will those poor calves be ready to travel this week?" Ellie asked.

"Sure and they will. They never give it thought. What's the matter, girl? You can't be feeling sorry for everything and everybody around here. This is a working ranch! You'd best hurry up

"Are you ready for the drive?" Aldon stood in front of the serving table, which had been brought outside for the noon meal.

"Ready when you are," she said, handing him a slice of bread. He laid it on top of his chili.

"Thanks for the grub." Aldon turned and walked over to a grove of

trees where the other men sat on the grass eating. She wished he could have stayed and talked, but she knew they must tend to their jobs. As Molly had said earlier, there was no time for lollygagging.

"We better slice the cakes." Molly came up behind her and set a cake and a knife on the table. "Those fellers will have all that chili et in no time and be looking for dessert."

She was right. They wolfed down their dinner, came for seconds, and then demolished the cakes. As the cooks cleared the tables, the men rested in the shade of the cottonwood trees with their hats pulled over their eyes. The younger ones, including Kenny Fitzgerald, roughhoused like warriors training for battle. *Too bad we have no young maidens here to swoon over them,* thought Ellie.

At suppertime, after the branding was finished, the men filed into the kitchen and seated themselves at the long table. Since she was going on the cattle drive, Aldon insisted that Ellie sit down with the men instead of serving. Molly gave him an annoyed look before she handed him the plate of Rocky Mountain Oysters. As the plate went around and the contents disappeared, the men laughed and joked. The plate was almost empty when it reached Ellie, but the men had stopped eating and talking and were staring at her. She forked a Rocky Mountain Oyster onto her plate, took a deep breath, and cut off a morsel. The men fell silent, all looking down the table at her. She knew she had to prove she wasn't a sissy in order to have their respect, so she put the bite into her mouth. As she chewed, she thought she might be sick again. It only took a moment, however, to discover that the meat tasted like nothing, but fried flour, salt, pepper, and beef.

She smiled, and the men around the table roared with approval.

CHAPTER 14

ALDON

Three days later, before sunrise, Aldon arranged himself on the seat of the chuck wagon with Ellie beside him. He was glad to have the use of Dieter's mules, as he slapped the reins lightly along their backs. Mules were good value. Maybe they weren't as pretty as horses, but they were stronger. They also had better horse-sense and enough self-respect not to allow folks to ride them to death.

"Git-up," he said as the animals pulled the wagon through the pasture and up toward the range. He looked at Ellie and she smiled at him just as sunshine suddenly rimmed the peaks.

The riders stayed in formation with the chuck-wagon in the lead. Joe, had three extra mounts on reins at the left while Dieter rode to the right. Several other cousins and uncles helped control the herd. Kenny rode behind them all in the lowliest position.

If we do this again next year, Aldon thought, *I'll give Kenny the job of wrangle. Once someone as bright and willing as he rides with the dust in his face, he deserves a promotion.*

As the group moved farther up the mountain, Aldon looked back at half a thousand bobbing heads. Cattle ranching had been good for his family, but if he had a choice, he'd rather be training quarter horses, except that the ranchers all trained their own. Next best thing might be to consider getting a job in Hollywoodland, like Bill.

"Well, Miss Morgan, here you are in the Wild West. What do you think of it?"

"I like it, but I'm going to have to get a hat. Where did you get yours?"

"For now there's one in the line-cabin you could use until we can get to town."

"I saw the sunbonnet on the shelf and tried it on. I should have worn it and been grateful, but it's just not my style. I like your John B. Stetson better; you think we could get one of those?" Ellie smoothed her hair, but the wind immediately blew mussed it again.

"You know the brand of my hat?" This gal was full of surprises.

"Morgan's department store carries them. I believe Mr. Stetson was inspired by the ten-gallon cowboy hats when he visited Colorado."

"You don't say?" Aldon thought she must be the smartest woman he'd ever met, except maybe for his mother, Nancy. "We'll get you one."

"By the way, thanks for letting me wear your mother's clothes. Are you sure she won't mind?" Ellie asked.

"Molly said Nancy would want you to wear anything she hadn't taken to Artesia. She figured you hadn't brought that kind of working duds." Aldon gave the mules another gentle slap with the reins to keep them going.

"This sheepskin is so warm and comfortable," she gave him a nudge with her shoulder.

He had given her the soft, leather jacket he'd grown out of when he was sixteen. Looking at her, he remembered how warm the wool lining felt when the temperature dropped and how the leather keep out the cold wind.

At first, the trail was wide enough, but soon it got so narrow that the herd no longer walked spread out but fell naturally into single file. They followed onto the shelf road with riders in between to make sure they didn't get scared. Aldon's ancestors had made the shelf road that went alongside one of the highest mountains by dynamiting a slice from it. It was a quicker and easier way than trying to drive the wagon over the boulders that hid beneath grass and wildflowers in the high meadows. Aldon knew the trail ran more than seventy feet above the creek in some places and was almost too narrow for the wagon, but the chance of the wagon sliding off had never worried him… before now.

Knowing that most Easterners got antsy about such heights he glanced at Ellie to see how she was doing. She stopped staring at the creek below long enough to lift questioning eyes to his.

"You see up there where the trees don't grow?" In order to distract her, he directed her attention to timberline.

"Yes. Did somebody cut them all down for firewood or what?" she asked searching the line of the peaks.

"No, it's too cold and dry for them to thrive up at that altitude."

"That's strange." She continued to look up.

"'I will lift up my eyes to the hills. My help comes from the Lord, who made heaven and earth,'" he murmured thoughtfully.

"What?" She seemed startled. "I wouldn't think you'd need much help. You can do anything."

"Oh, I've got my problems," he said. "But when I think about my friend, they fade away. I've needed to know that a lot since I got home from the war."

She gave him such an eager look that he wondered if he should tell her more. He'd try it and if she lost interest, he'd quit.

"For one thing, I sometimes need help holding my temper. It might have something to do with the way my brothers and I always fought when we were coming up. We only had to look at each other cross-eyed and we were in a tangle. I thought I'd grown out of that, but it seems the anger has come back."

"Everybody has faults of one kind or another." Ellie slipped her arm through his. "I think you're a good man."

"Thank you ma'am, but I wouldn't mind being a bit more saintly."

"Nobody is a saint," she said.

"I beg to differ, kid. In the Bible, followers of Christ are called saints."

"Why?"

"I don't know," he shrugged. Suddenly, he decided that he'd said enough. He had her respect, why risk losing it by being preachy.

By noontime, they arrived at a high, wide meadow ringed with shimmering aspens. Bunch grass, Indian paintbrush, and daisies covered the ground, and fleecy clouds floated lazy against the blue sky. A cooling breeze rolled past on its way down the mountainside. As the riders stopped the forward motion a few cows lay down while others foraged as their calves nursed.

CHAPTER 15

ALDON

When supper was over and the clean-up finished, Aldon decided to hike up to the beaver pond for a bath. He grabbed a bar of Molly's homemade soap, got a towel, and clean clothes from his saddlebag, and joined Joe and Dieter on the trail. At the pond, the men raced to see who could get into the water first. Joe had to stop and help Dieter get his boots off, so Aldon made the big splash. He started swimming as fast as he could in the icy water, all the time wishing for the tepid water between the hot and cold spring of his regular pond. He was half way across by the time Joe jumped in, and Dieter came next. The three of them wrestled over the soap like kids. When Aldon finally got hold of it, he washed quickly and then threw the soap to Joe. He got out, and while the two struggled again, he dried off and put on fresh jeans and a flannel shirt, and strapped on his sidearm. For a while, he sat on the large, flat boulder that made a platform at the edge of the water. Still warm from the sun, the rock, felt so good he wanted to lie down and go to sleep right then. He took a deep breath of clean, pine-scented air, held it and released the weariness of the trail with a sigh of satisfaction. They had arrived with all the men, the woman, the horses, dogs, and cattle safe.

When the men got back to camp, Aldon found Ellie sitting on the chuck wagon tailgate with her head against the post that supported the canopy. She looked so hot and dusty, he felt sorry for her.

"No more travel until tomorrow when we leave the cattle and ride back down to the ranch," he said.

"Any chance of my getting a bath, too?" Ellie slid off the tailgate and stood looking up at him in the gathering dusk.

"Sure." Aldon swallowed hard at the thought of Ellie taking a bath anywhere, but this was practically out in public. He'd need to go with her and keep her safe, but who would keep him safe from the strange feelings he'd been having lately. He shook the thoughts away. After all, bringing Ellie along was his idea and that made her his responsibility.

"You sure it's okay? I don't want to be any trouble." Her shoulders sagged.

"Come with me." Aldon felt heat in his face and chastised himself. Blushing was for women and children, but he hadn't been able to break himself of it yet. While he found another towel, Ellie retrieved a bundle of clothes from the wagon.

"You need a packhorse?" he quipped.

"I have to have clean clothes; I can't stand these another minute." As they ascended the trail with Aldon in the lead, he stopped, turned, and took the clothing.

"I am perfectly capable of being my own packhorse, thank you." She tugged at the armful. He held on.

"The trail is rocky. Since it's new to you, I'd better carry them in case you need to grab a bush or something to steady yourself." He moved on.

As they arrived at the pool, they heard a splash and saw several beavers glide away toward a mound of brush. Aldon helped Ellie step up on the boulder, and then pointed out the sights.

"The beavers live over there," he explained, indicating the far side where a pile of branches stuck up at the edge of the water.

"Yes?" Ellie waited for more.

"It's called a beaver lodge," he continued. "They swim under the woven sticks and into a warm, dry den. See the pointed stumps over there?" She nodded and he went on. "Beavers cut the saplings down with their teeth in order to use them for making the lodge. They also eat the spongy wood beneath the bark."

"No wonder people say *busy as a beaver*," she said. "Imagine having to chew down a tree before you can eat breakfast." They both chuckled.

"Beavers mate for life," he looked at her then cast his gaze out over the pond.

"Do they? That's good, like people," she nodded.

"I'll sit on this rock. You get in the water. Here's the soap." He handed it to her. "I promise I won't look. The water is so cold; you won't want to stay in long."

Aldon heard Ellie's soft whimper as she undressed, then heard a squeal of outrage, as she stepped into the freezing water. After a few minutes, he stretched out on the warm rock and listened to her humming a hurried song. Why hadn't he thought to heat water on the campfire and let her bathe inside the cabin?

"Coming out," she said waking him from a short nap. He got the towel and laid it over her shoulders with his head turned away. He wanted to share the warmth of his body by putting his arms around her, but knew it would be the act of a cad. He hoped holding her by the shoulders would help.

"You can turn loose now," she said. When he did not obey she shook him off. "Let me go, you big lug. You're squashing me so I can hardly breathe." Realizing that he had been tightening his grip instead of turning loose, He let go.

"I'm sorry," he apologized. "Let's hurry now. I'm going over there on the other side of the boulder while you finish getting dressed."

CHAPTER 16

ALDON

"The guys seem to be out for the night, but I'm not ready to sleep, yet, are you?" Aldon asked.

"No, how would you feel about playing some music, this is if you don't think it will wake them."

"Once those guys crawl into their bedrolls, nothing short of a stampede could get them up. Come on, we'll go get our instruments." He took her to the chuck wagon and found her violin case and his mandolin. "You can take these, if you will, and I'll get the chairs from the cabin. We'll play for the man in the moon."

"We've never played together before." He set the old chairs a ways off from the sleeping ring, and Ellie arranged herself with her violin at the ready. What shall we play?"

"Turkey in the Straw!" He concentrated on tuning his mandolin and then struck up a chord. She followed easily as the song got fast, faster, and fastest. Until…their fingers tripped and they broke down laughing.

Aldon strummed chords and sensing a chance for improvisation, Ellie found notes that blended in. He wondered if there were anything she couldn't do with a fiddle. At the end of the song, a loud snore came from the circle around the campfire.

"That must have been a vote of approval," Aldon said with a chuckle.

Ellie began to play something soft and haunting, something Aldon had never heard before. He set his mandolin against the leg of his chair and closed his eyes so he could listen with all his mind and heart. What richness and depth she added to the moonlit night. At first, it was like an ancient Irish melody exploring every corner of his soul. Later, it danced between joy and sadness, putting him in a place where he felt fully contented with an occasional edge of yearning that pierced him to the soul.

The high peaks against the evening sky, the shimmer of moon, and the soft flap of a white owl overhead put a sheen on his happiness. He surveyed his mountains, his cabin, his neighbors around the fire, and this woman playing the violin like a master. But, Ellie was not *his* woman, she was only the most beautiful and exciting female he had ever known. When the piece ended, the night was silent except for the lowing of a cow in the meadow.

Ellie sighed. She rose and without a word, put her violin away, walked across the clearing, and entered the cabin.

Ellie

Ellie entered a room bathed in moonlight. The tang of vinegar assailed her sense of smell, and she wondered if someone, such as Kenny, had cleaned the space while she and Aldon were at the pond. She spotted a kerosene lamp with a Prince Albert can lying beside it. Grandad had told her how you had to keep *Lucifer sticks* dry in tin cans, so she opened it and found what she was looking for. She removed the lamp's shining glass chimney, turned up the wick, and struck the match against a rough corner of the table.

She walked across the small room to a cot covered with a blue and white, star-patterned quilt. What a work of art! Grandmother could sell a quilt like this for an excellent price in the city.

Ellie heard a gentle tap on the cabin door, and when she opened it, Aldon stood there with the chairs from outside.

"Let me put these where they belong and light the fire. Will you be okay?" he asked his voice gentle. "Is the cabin clean?"

"Yes, everything's fine. Thank you for taking such good care of me."

"You don't ever have to thank me," he said shaking his head. When Aldon finished his small chores, Ellie closed the door behind him and went to the four-paned window to watch him walk away. *It's too bad I couldn't have asked him to stay so we could talk*, she thought. *But what would the men have thought?* She turned the wick so that the light went out, then walked to the bed by the light of the moon.

At the edge of sleep, Ellie saw herself drifting over a misty pond. Then she was no longer alone. She was pounding the arm that held her... Aldon's arm. She felt no sense of panic or fear. She just didn't want to be held back. She drifted into a dream about a white owl flying through the night making whooshing sounds with its big wings.

The next morning when Aldon rapped on the door, Ellie felt as if she'd just fallen into bed. She snuggled down and pulled the heavy goose-down pillow over her head.

I've brought you some warmer clothes." Aldon said opening the door slightly, "I'll lay them here.

"It's not morning yet," she called. There was no answer. He had gone away, and knowing it was her duty to get up and help Kenny cook breakfast for the men, she forced her feet onto the cold floor. For a moment, her mind went back to France during the war where everyone suffered cold and hunger. The sounds of men getting up brought back memories of snow on the shoulders of her military cape as she changes bandages and comforted dying men. She hadn't shirked then, and she wouldn't shirk now.

With her arms wrapped around herself, she hurried to the pile of folded clothes and put on long-johns, stockings, trousers, a too large, hand-knit sweater, and boots. She added Aldon's sheepskin jacket, which had become her favorite item of clothing.

When she got to the main campfire, she and Kenny prepared bacon, eggs, flapjacks, and left-over beans. When the cattle had all been seen to, Aldon joined her on the chuck wagon seat. This time he asked her to drive.

CHAPTER 17

ELLIE

The wagon swayed as Aldon took the reins to drive the mules onto the shelf road. He and Ellie were returning home the way they had come. Their only other choice was to pick their way over a meadow strewn with rocks and runoff channels, either dried or filled with water, and Aldon had said the obstructions were camouflaged by grasses and wildflowers, and could trap a wheel or a hoof in an instant.

They arrived at the ranch at four o'clock in the afternoon. Ellie was looking forward to a bath, and maybe a short rest, so Aldon let her off at the door saying he would unhitch the mules and take them home to Joe's family.

When Ellie entered the kitchen, Molly was waiting for somebody to talk to about the day's work.

"We caught three fat hens and butchered them. We saved the feathers for pillows. We dredged the chicken pieces in eggs and flour and fried them. Now wait," she held up her hand when she saw that Ellie was losing interest. "That's not all. We brought a peck of potatoes in from the root cellar and peeled, cut, cooked and mashed them. We're bushed. Kate's resting and I need your help finishing the supper."

At six-o'clock, the back door opened and in came Aldon and Kenny.

"It's about time you got here. Supper's ready." Molly said looking at Aldon, her eyes soft with love. Ellie was reminded that Molly had never married or had children and was glad she had helped with Aldon and his brothers and that she had family. She was a good woman at heart, and she had helped to turn him into a special kind of man.

The cowboy took Molly into his arms and waltzed her around the small expanse of linoleum. As they passed the stove, Aldon paused to admire the chicken and to peer into the pot of boiling potatoes.

"Yep," Molly said grinning, all your favorites, fried chicken, peas in cream sauce with new onions and mashed taters.

"Molly is the best cook in the world." He shot a glance at Ellie who smiled and nodded at his exuberance.

"Now, who's been kissin' the Blarney stone?" Molly put her head down, trying to look modest, but when she looked up, her shining eyes showed her joy.

"You've mentioned that *Blarney Stone* before, but I never thought to ask what it was." Aldon said.

"I do believe it's about buttering people up. I hear you go to Blarney Castle and lie down and lean backward over a big hole and kiss the ancient stone embedded in the wall, then you get the gift o' gab. My family just says that. None of them has been in Ireland for over a hundred years so it may mean something else altogether." As Molly bustled over to check on the peas, the door from the dining room swung open and young Mr. Enrico walked in.

He came straight to Ellie, grabbed her hand, and kissed it. "*Ciao, Signorina,* how are you? Please tell me about your adventure." He continued to hold her hand.

Looking at Aldon, Ellie caught sight of a scowl that would make a dog crawl under the table. When he realized she was reacting to his dour expression, he forced a smile.

"Come on Kenny; let's get washed up for supper." The screen door banged behind them, and Ellie heard their footsteps going up the stairs attached to the side of the house.

"Signora Solano wants Aldon, Ellie, and the bambina to eat with us in the dining room." Enrico dropped Ellie's hand. "She says we will talk about the musicale she is planning. The Fitzgerald boy will remain in the kitchen with the rest of the help."

"Yes, Sir," Molly said, her eyes narrowed in resentment. Ellie knew she must have been looking forward to having Aldon and Kenny to herself at the supper table so she could hear about the *adventure*.

"Check what we need in there." Molly told her.

When Ellie came back, she reported that the Signora wanted them to serve tea right away and that they needed to seat Seraphina tall enough so she'd be able to feed herself.

"Tea!" Molly put her fists on her hips and shook her head. "

Not knowing what else to do, Ellie stood waiting for more instructions.

"Oh, stack some books in a chair and cover them with a towel for the bairn. Her highness wants to train her to be a great lady. That's probably the reason for the tea party. I'll put the kettle on, and you see to the cups and saucers. When you finish, go ahead and get into your prettiest dress. You're dining with royalty tonight."

"All I have is my suit skirt and blouse, or one of my work dresses.

"Oh, I'd say the blue skirt and white shirtwaist would do quite well. They like to dress up and that's the best you have, which is plenty good enough." Molly grabbed a dishtowel, wrapped it around the handle of the iron skillet, and slid it into the warming oven.

CHAPTER 18

ELLIE

It seems good to keep an account of my Western adventure, so I bought a little book at the general store and this will be my first entry.

The latest news is that Signora has asked me to call her *Lia*. It's her Christian name and she says we are best girl*friends* now, but it's difficult to think of her as one of my employers and a best friend at the same time.

Lia, Enrico and I spend a lot of time doing nothing which makes me feel guilty because I'm still getting paid, yet others have to do the real work I was hired to do. I've been helping in one way or another since I was old enough to stand on a chair and wash dishes. I have worked in the beauty salon. I have run errands and written letters. I have done every job in the store except unloading trucks. I drove an ambulance at the front. Not working is making me feel useless, and I can tell Molly is unhappy about it too.

Lia has me wake her at ten with breakfast in bed. She then wants me to discuss clothing and jewelry so she will look pretty for her step-grandson, when he comes to her suite to "spend" the day. When she is dressed to the nines, I'm to go and knock on his door and wake him. While he stays in bed, I lay out his clothes, which I don't think is proper. I then go to the kitchen to prepare his breakfast and bring it up to Lia's suite. At night, he keeps late hours away from the house. I don't know where he goes or how he gets there, but he must have found something to do in this small community. Most of the day Signor is in his office, or walking out-of-doors with Aldon. Molly says he's getting much better now. She and Kate, with Seraphina keep the household going.

Enrico and Lia play romantic opera records. Enrico was named for the great Caruso and takes his naming seriously. He has a degree in singing and music and thinks he will be an American opera star someday. I think perhaps Enrico has had too much experience with women. After lunch we drink a little champagne and play jazz records. Lia insists that we dance. Enrico exudes an air of relaxed sensuality that puts me into such a lethargy that the only time I come alive is when he takes me in his arms and we dance. None of this is right or useful in any way. I feel embarrassed and ashamed, but I don't know how to get out of that room. It's as if I'm being held in a tower like Rapunzel. I need a prince to break me out.

The records they play affect me as well. Grandmother took Mother and me to the opera many times, and when I hear Verdi and Puccini on Lia's Victrola I fall in love with the composers over and over again and perhaps a little in love with Enrico. I don't know.

It's not as if the room were a dark bistro. Lia, being a painter, loves splashes of light and shadow. She calls them *chiaroscuro*. That is why she arranges the curtains and dressing screens to provide a changing French Impressionist painting inside the suite. I must admit it is beautiful. When I go down to help Molly with supper, she grouses about my lay-about ways. I have to admit that my daytime activities do verge on debauchery. I have no idea where it will end.

Enrico and Lia are like small children wanting the constant attention of an adult, and for some reason, I've been elected the adult. Lia ordered jazz records from the Sears Roebuck catalog and I have been teaching them the Charleston and the Black-Bottom. She reads magazines with beautiful fashion photographs and interesting gossip columns.

"Please, Ellie," Lia said one day as Enrico stepped away to put on a new record, "I want to be a flapper like you. Will you cut my hair?"

"I don't think of myself as a flapper." I objected. "But I will be glad to style your hair."

"I do not mean to insult you. I want only to be *Modern Millie* for my Giovanni," she pouted. "Before bed, he sits in my rocking chair, his legs in their fine trousers stretched into the middle of the room. He watches me brush my hair. He says, 'Oh, Lia, your hair is so long, and so curly.' But he cares not a whit that it is heavy and hot. When he leaves to go to his own bed, he gives me a small kiss on the cheek. I feel then, like an abandoned rose in a garden of love. I sit in the chair where he has sat and look out at millions of diamonds in a black silk sky, then I lie down in my bed alone.

I was taken aback. It seemed all her thoughts were of her husband. That was good, but it made her behavior with Enrico all the more puzzling.

"You do have wonderful hair. Surely, Signor will object if we cut it. I turned her so I could study the natural curls that cascaded to her waist. "I didn't bring my hair cutting tools from the beauty salon. Can you wait until I send for them?"

"No, no, no, it must be cut this moment. I am sick to death and perishing from the heat. Look," she parted the curtain of hair so I could see the redness on the back of her neck. "Heat rash is it not?" she demanded.

"Yes, you're right. You'll be much more comfortable with it short and you will look just as pretty. I wonder where we could get a razor."

"Let's go. We'll be back in a while, Enrico," Lia grabbed me and pulled me toward the door. "Aldon has a razor. I saw it in the barn when I was with him."

"You...?"

"Come, along, Aldon's riding fence today, he will not miss a little borrow." She grabbed a comb and headed for the door, and I followed, stunned. Aldon and Lia? No, it couldn't be.

"We can't go into Aldon's quarters and take his razor without asking," I said, as I followed her down the hallway.

"Oh, pooh, come, do not do the dawdle." She waved her hand in dismissal of my scruples.

"We will stop at the pump and wet your hair, so I can cut it with a razor." That was all I knew to say.

CHAPTER 19

ELLIE

When we climbed to the loft, the barn cat met us and twined around our ankles. The space was small but tidy with a built in cot and a small desk. A shelf attached to the wall held the razor Lia was looking for. The mirror above it gave back a cloudy reflection and I immediately decided to ask Grandmother to send a new one in a silver frame. Aldon deserved it.

"Let us cut." Lia said, handing me the razor.

"I wonder why Aldon has such old-fashioned shaving equipment." I opened the razor. "During the war, the Gillette Company issued safety razors to all military men and then everybody started using them." Lia didn't seem interested so I swished the blade back and forth on a razor strop hanging from a nail on the wall —swoosh-swish until I sensed it was sharp enough to cut some of Lia's hair. I knew I'd have to sharpen it again before we finished.

"Aldon is – how you say – sentimental," Lia answered. "The shaving equipment was his great grandfather's." Once again, I wondered how she knew so much about the man's personal life.

We moved the desk chair to the middle of the floor, and Lia sat down. I began by parting off sections of her hair to work on. The razor had been sharpened so many times that the edge was thin and sharp. At the first stroke, Lia started talking. That always happened in a beauty salon the minute you got someone in the chair. We stylists had been trained to listen like amateur Freuds without much comment or advice.

"I learned to pick grapes when I was five-years-old," Lia mused aloud. She paused to watch me drape the first long strand of dark wavy hair over a hay bale. I was glad she didn't panic when I started as so many others had when their life-long growth of hair was assaulted. I hoped Signor Solano would be as happy as she was about it.

"Papa taught me to work hard when we lived on the Solano estate." Lia went on. "Papa was their vineyard manager. His parents were dead and he had no sisters or brothers. My job was to play with Signor and Signora's grandson, Enrico. We were the same age. No matter what we did, his grandparents never got angry because he was their prince. But when we slid down the banisters and landed in the potted plants we got dirt all over the floors and the servants found sneaky ways to punish us. They would hide our favorite toys, or bribe the cook to hold back dessert. Without me Enrico would have been a lonely, small boy and without him, I was only a fat child."

When I started to protest, she held up her hand to stop me. "But my mama and my papa loved me."

As she talked, I cut and laid locks of hair in a line along the edge of a bale. As I looked at the shiny treasure, I realized her hair would make a beautiful wig and probably some postiches. Grandmother had made sure I had classes in wig-weaving so I could fill orders. I was a qualified *posticheur*.

"Would you like to have a wig for special occasions?" I asked Lia, pausing in my cutting.

"No, I want never to see all these hair again."

"You might want longer hair arranged for dress-up occasions."

"I might want longer hair if Signor is too disappointed that I have cut it. Yes, you may make me a wig. I will pay you for it, but I don't know if I will wear it. What I truly want is a marcelled bob like I have seen in the magazines."

"All right, that will be easy with your naturally wavy hair. And thank you, I will work on the wig in the evenings. I'll send for my equipment right away." I was excited. There was nothing more soothing than tying wigs. It would be a good way to support myself when I grew old, that was if I didn't end up in the department store. I'd have to mind my manners to make sure that didn't come to pass.

"Now let us change the story. I am looking forward to the grand musicale," She looked up at me. "Will that not be *divertimento*?"

"Diverting, yes, it will be fun," I said. "I hope Aldon won't be angry about our using his razor. I'll leave it sharpened when we're finished."

CHAPTER 20

ALDON

Dear Mr. Cameron, Mrs. Cameron, and Mrs. Morgan

How do you do? It's good to meet Ellie's family even if it's just in a letter. I hope all of you are in good health and prospering. You have a fine daughter and granddaughter in Ellie, who has certainly made a place for herself here. This morning, she asked me to write you about my wartime adventures. She thought her grandfather, particularly, might be interested in them. There isn't much to tell, but I'm happy to tell what there is.

I flew a *Nieuport Bebe* in France. It was retrofitted with camera equipment so we could take photographs of what the enemy was doing. By the time the war ended, I was twenty-five. Because not many fliers or photographers survived to that age, the younger men called me, *The Old Man.* I didn't mind.

We were billeted in a small chateau in a pear orchard away from the front. It was spring, and my window framed clusters of white blossoms on the trees outside. My room had a linoleum floor, a chifferobe for clothes, a table and chair, and a lantern. The bed was lumpy, but a feather quilt (they called it a duvet) came in handy for cold nights. We slept whenever we got the chance. Doc said it was the only way to get our energy back after being in danger for such long hours.

I did wish they had a horse or two around there. I could have ridden or spent some time working with them. By that time, they'd all been eaten, though. I was sad about that. I understand the French still eat horse meat. I guess you'd have to develop a taste for it, and forget you'd had several best friends who happened to be horses.

I missed my family while I was gone, but they wrote and sent packages when they could. Ma and my Aunt Molly knit a lot of socks and what they called balaclavas for the soldiers, and I got my share of those. I guess about everybody knows what a balaclava is, but in case you don't, it's a warm cap that comes down over your ears and up onto your chin. In case you're wondering what I did with them all, I passed them around. A good, thick balaclava can come in handy in the wintertime.

Ma and Molly also sent a homemade cake packed in popcorn. By the time we opened the package, the popcorn had been smashed into the cake. We ate it anyhow and the boys went crazy over it. I'll bet they never got another one like it.

Many pilots started out as photographers. I hear tell that the Red Baron fellow started out as a photographer before he became an ace fighter pilot. Most of us had only seen a camera once or twice. We had a lot to learn, but our lack of knowledge didn't count against us. They constantly changed out the equipment and we had to figure out how to use it.

When I became a pilot they kept me in surveillance. In Belgium, my passenger could hardly find anything to take pictures of. The countryside was desolate as far as you could see. Once in a while you might catch the stump of a burned tree or a bombed out building, but most of the landscape was just wet mud or dried mud – not much variety in that.

I'm thinking the following is the story Ellie wanted me to tell. If it was a school essay, I suppose I'd entitle it, "My Closest Call." It happened while the photographer and I were flying behind the lines. The place hadn't been destroyed yet, but the Huns were doing their worst. Our engine started sputtering, so I shut it off and looked for a place to land. It was quiet then — just us and the wind whistling past our ears. We lost altitude fast, so I decided to set down in a field. That all went fine until the bus picked a downhill slope and flipped when it landed. We were upside down with two wings broken by the time we stopped sliding. Fortunately, the bus did not blow up — probably because Somebody reminded me to turn off the gas. A group of resistance folk saw us coming down and got us out of the airplane and into a barn *tuit de suite* as they say in France, *toot sweet*. The next thing I knew, the Bebe was hidden under a sort of haystack. They didn't have much vegetation, but they put canvas and branches over it so no one could spot it from the air.

They brought us stew with plenty of turnips and not much meat and were we ever glad for it. They got word to our side right away. A crew came in a big truck and hauled us and the Bebe back to base. I kept on flying and even taught a few pilots until the war ended. That's it for now.

Come on out to Colorado and see us. Come in the fall if you can, the quaking aspen is most colorful at round-up time. Would you like to go on round-up with us? I promise you wouldn't have to ride drag.

CHAPTER 21

ELLIE

The sun had not yet risen when Ellie and Aldon met in the kitchen on Ellie's birthday, June 21. They had fallen into the habit of starting their days together before they went to their jobs.

"Well, today's your birthday and I have a surprise. Kenny and I have will take you up into the range and see about getting you a wild mustang to train. "Excitement sparkled in Aldon's eyes. "Man, do I ever love chasing those beautiful animals and bringing them home."

"But doesn't it mean you're breaking up a family?" Ellie asked.

"In a way, but after foals grow up, they don't seem to pay much attention to their dams. They're okay as long as they can be with other horses or something. And we've got to keep the herd culled so that it doesn't over-populate the range. Any land can only support so many large animals or even small ones for that matter. I say let's cull a few and give some people the pleasure of riding them. Or we can send them out to Hollywoodland. Bill says they can become movie stars"

After they'd left the kitchen as tidy as they'd found it, they went out to the barn. From there, they heard Kenny's motorcycle roaring up the drive, and went out to meet him.

"Get a horse," Aldon joked. Kenny waved happily and went on his way to saddle the horse he always rode when he came to the ranch.

~

Aldon took the lead as they made their way up the side of the mountain to the line cabin and beyond to the first stand of aspens where he expected to see the mustangs. The first one Ellie saw was a palomino standing apart from the rest of the herd guarding her colt. Close by, with heads bent to graze, were forty or so others in a variety of colors from sorrel to the browns, blacks, and whites of appaloosas.

"There he is, that black stallion with the main herd." When Aldon leaned over to speak to Ellie, the leather of his saddle creaked slightly; and the stallion raised his head and sniffed. As quick as the wind, he bolted followed by the herd, which made a river of horses flowing through the meadow and down the slope of the mountain. Aldon and Kenny took after them immediately while Ellie looked on. As soon as she realized what was happening, she nudged Ribbons with her boot heels.

Aldon and Kenny drove the wild herd into a narrow box canyon at the end of which the family had built a rough corral.

Before going into the enclosure the lead stallion suddenly reversed and led the herd back past their would-be captors. The palomino which had been trying to keep up with the herd with her baby paused. Kenny and Aldon lassoed her and their horses dug in so that she could not get away. Once she realized she was caught, she began to whinny, rear and twist. Her colt danced out of the way, while Ellie admired his golden coat, his white mane and his energy.

Back at the line-cabin, the colt and mare went easily into the small corral and after he was unsaddled, Chief sauntered over to inspect them.

Ellie recalled what Aldon had told her about horses. He'd said that they needed to be with other animals — almost any creatures from dogs to goats to humans would do. A human was preferable to no company at all. Ellie thought such neediness put the animals at a disadvantage, but the knowledge of it touched a deep place in her soul and she knew she was needy too. She could hardly wait to get to know the pair of them. It was the best birthday she had ever had.

CHAPTER 22

ALDON

When they got home the next morning, they led the horses down from the line cabin then did their regular chores. Kenny put his horse away and went back to town to help his folks with their many enterprises.

That night, Aldon dropped onto his bed in the loft and slept like a dog. By five a. m., he was shaved and ready to meet Ellie in the kitchen. Today would be different. They would shorten their coffee time and head for the corral where he would show her how he trained them.

He mentally thanked Molly's *Daddo,* which is what she called her grandfather, who had taught the Leitzinger sons about the large beasts. Once they'd learned all he could teach them, he called them *Sullivans* after a relative of his, the first known horse whisperer in Ireland long ago. Asking Ellie to wait outside the corral, Aldon went into the barn to get the palominos. When he shooed them out, they trotted to the other side of the corral and stood shuffling their feet and looking at him.

He checked to see where Ellie was and was impressed with how well the golden color of the Palominos matched Ellie's blond beauty. At that moment he wanted nothing more than to stand and stare at her like a love struck youth, but he knew Ellie would rather have him get on with the job at hand. Suddenly he knew how important it was to him make Ellie happy. *Whatever she wants*, he thought, *she gets. Now and always.*

Aldon took a long, thin rope from his pocket, and holding one end began tossing the other end at the mare. As it floated toward her, she began to canter around the inside of the corral trying to stay away from it. The colt followed. Aldon knew that instinct compelled them to run first and look back later to see what was chasing them.

As he circled slowly and watched the animals, music began to play in Aldon's head as it so often did when he was working. The song this time was, "The Emperor's Waltz, a perfect three-quarter rhythm for the canter. He had learned it from one of the few records Nancy bought for the wind-up Victrola. No one else in his family had this strange quirk, but he enjoyed the tunes his mind served up, they always seemed appropriate somehow. It must be the *sub-conscious* he had learned about in an extra course he took at agricultural college that caused it.

Never having been abused by man, the mare and her colt had nothing to unlearn. As he shortened his line to let them come closer to him, the dam slowed down and started licking her lips and making chewing motions. She dropped her head which told him that she was looking for a friend now, someone to help her in a terrifying situation. It was time to put the line away along with his aggressive stance and become more approachable. He turned his back, let his shoulders slump slightly, and became a figure of welcome and comfort. The less attention he gave her the closer she came. He turned sideways ignoring her, but one of her ears twisted in his direction showing she was aware of his presence and valued it. She touched Aldon's back with her nose.

He shifted into a slow turn to face the horse and then scratched the long bone of her nose and told her what a good girl she was. In a moment, he quietly asked Ellie to bring the rope halter to him. She nodded and came into the corral to give it to him. He slipped it over the horse's head and handed the end to Ellie.

"She's all yours, happy birthday. Walk her around," he said. Ellie's eyes widened and she gave him a delighted smile. He knew she couldn't speak for fear of startling the horse, but it didn't matter. He had a warm feeling in his chest knowing he had accomplished his goal.

CHAPTER 23

ALDON

One day Molly came out of Signor's office to tell Aldon the master wanted to see him. When he opened the door, Signor Solano motioned for him to be seated. "Aldon, I have ordered a Packard Six automobile for Father Contenti and I want you to go to Denver on the train and bring it home.

Yes, sir. I'll be glad to do that. Is it all right if I go on Friday?" At Signor Solano's nod, Aldon rose and turned to leave. Then he paused and turned back. "Sir," he said, "Miss Ellie is looking tired. I think she'd enjoy a rest from her work here. Would it be all right if I took her along? I'll be staying at the Cattleman's, but she could stay somewhere else for the sake of propriety."

After Signor Solano gave his permission with a knowing smile, Aldon hurried to ask Ellie to go to Denver with him. It didn't take much to persuade her, but she refused to admit that she needed to get away. The whole plan changed when Lia heard about the jaunt. She invited herself and Enrico along so they could all shop for clothes to wear to Molly's birthday party and to the Rodeo Dance on the Fourth of July. Lia said Aldon could stay at the Cattleman's Hotel if he wished, but the rest of them would be at the Brown Derby, the best hotel in Colorado.

The train left Clifton at seven on a Friday morning. Aldon talked

the conductor into letting him and Ellie stand out on the caboose platform so they would have a good view of the highest suspension bridge
in the world as the train went under it in the Royal Gorge canyon

"Hey, kid," Aldon said, as they braced themselves against the sway
of the train. "What will you name your horses?"

"How about Susie Q for the mare? That's what my granddad called
me instead of Ellie."

"Susie Q, huh. Yeah, I like it. How about the colt?"

"I think Horace," she said with a giggle.

"Horace the horse?" he shook his head.

"Yes, after Horace Greely whom you could say is the reason I'm
here." Ellie laughed and then he could tell she was joking with him.

"Seriously." He said.

"I don't know, can you think of a good name for him?"

"How about Pike for the explorer who discovered Pike's Peak."

"Hmm, I guess it'll do. We'll try it out, but if I don't like it I don't
have to keep it." She tossed her head in such a way that he wondered if
she might be flirting with him.

"Yeh," he said. "If you don't like it, you don't have to keep it. I
somehow got the idea you were a bit afraid of horses. You won't ever
be afraid of him, will you?"

"Oh, no. But I was afraid when I first got here. "Ellie dipped her
head then looked up into his eyes. "The first one I ever rode ran away
with me and I got hurt. After that, I thought I'd stay away from
horses."

"I noticed you kind of like your mare and colt, though. Do you …
like them all right?"

"I don't just like them, I love them. You're so good to go to all that
trouble to catch them and then give them to me."

"You're a natural. I have some more things to teach you." Joy
surged through him. "Pike will hardly need training when he grows
up." Aldon slipped his arm around Ellie's shoulders. He intended to
give her a quick, one-armed hug, but the train lurched throwing him
back against the caboose. When Ellie got off balance, he braced
himself and tightened his arms around her so the two of them wouldn't
fall. The minute she reached around him, a blend of peace and pleasure flowed through him like hot coffee on a cold morning. Wait a

minute, though. She had regained her balance and still she leaned into him.

As soon as she realized what she was doing, she pulled away. But the warmth stayed with him.

"Thank you for catching me, and thank you for teaching us." She took a deep breath.

By this time they were out of the canyon and heading east toward Artesia. When the train swept past the Colorado State Penitentiary where some of the worst criminals in the West were incarcerated, Aldon thought about Cookie and his wife and granddaughter.

"I heard that Kate's husband ended up in that prison," Ellie remarked.

"Yes, he was here, but he's gone now."

"What happened?"

"Cookie Fisher was a good man," Aldon said. I told you he helped on cattle pushes and round-ups. His real job was at the saloon where he was treated like a slave. He saved money to send for Kate and Seraphina and enough to build a cabin but it was time for Slick Sam's yearly visit to Clifton."

"Slick? That's a strange name."

"Not if you knew Slick," he said. "He was a traveling gambler. People knew he cheated, but somehow he always managed to find a sucker to invite to the table. Cookie wanted to buy Kate furniture for the cabin so he bet his stake on a Royal Flush and lost. He knew Slick was a cheat, knew he'd made a big mistake playing, but It was apparently the last humiliation he was going to stand for. The day after the game, he made a separate pot of chili for the gambler."

"Poison?" Ellie asked.

"Yep. But I've got this to say for him, he put in enough so that Slick didn't suffer long. My friend Sheriff Oates came up from Artesia to arrest him. After Cookie was tried, he was the first to try out the new electric chair."

"Oh, poor Kate. She must be grieving so… I thought she was just standoffish." Ellie put her hand on Aldon's sleeve as if to comfort him. Aldon nodded and covered her hand with his until she drew away.

When the train pulled into the station, Aldon walked Ellie, Lia, and Enrico to a taxi. He held Ellie back for a moment. "I'm going to pick up the automobile then I'll come get you and we can go to dinner. I'd like it to be just the two of us."

"Could I come with you now?" Ellie asked. He thought he heard a longing in her voice.

"You'd better ask the Signora, we don't want her mad," he answered. He went around to ask the driver to wait and in a moment Ellie was at his side telling him Lia wanted her to wait until after shopping the next day to go to dinner with Aldon.

CHAPTER 24

ELLIE

As the taxi drew up to the hotel, Ellie couldn't help a sigh of relief at being surrounded by tall buildings and noisy traffic. She loved the mountains and the clear fresh air in the valley, but she supposed most people felt more at home in the kind of place where they grew up.

Denver, the capitol of Colorado was growing fast. She could hardly believe that when it came time to choose a capitol, one of the small towns in the Wet Mountain Valley had lost the designation by only one vote. Just think, if it had won, it would be the city, now and maybe Denver would be the almost abandoned ghost town. At the hotel, bell-boys carried the luggage to the third-story bedrooms assigned to the three of them.

Ellie's room had a large double bed with art-deco designs in the duvet and pillows. A window looked out over the busy street. She went into the tiled bathroom and washed her face with a generously sized, pristine-white wash-cloth.

The evening went quickly, the four of them ate at the hotel when Aldon came and everyone, except Enrico seemed to want to go to bed early. After Lia left, Aldon and Ellie sat lobby talking for a while, then Aldon left and Ellie went up to her room again.

~

The next morning, a knock came at the door, and when Ellie opened it, Lia swept into the room, walked straight to the window, and stood looking down at the traffic.

"Are you ready to go shopping, now? Enrico is waiting." Lia had changed into a light summer dress. The skirt floated out as she turned back to Ellie. "He is excited to get his measure for the new suit. He wants a black fedora, two ties, shirts, and I believe I will buy him a set of diamond cuff-links. What do you think of that? I did not want to wear any of my old hats. They would not fit now that my hair is cut. We will select a new one first thing straw, I think. We will tell them to throw the old one away."

"Am I all right like this?" Ellie asked. She was wearing the same blue serge suit she'd traveled in." Looking at Lia's airy voile made her feel hot and uncomfortable by comparison.

"Oh, poof, you are, of course, fine. For it will be a new dress, of the soft cotton like mine. The suit will be sent here in a box. You must have also a light summer jacket for evenings. We will buy dresses for Molly's birthday party and for the Independence Day Dance. No one in the valley has ever seen such as we will be in our finery. Come now." She led the way to the elevator and they went down to meet Enrico in the lobby.

"Please go ahead," Ellie said as they walked past a bank. "I'll catch up with you at the store. I assume you'll be in men's outfitters or ladies apparel?" She nodded first at Enrico who stood in his soiled white suit with his hair falling over the collar of the jacket. "They may have a barber shop."

"Oh yes," said Lia. "He will have a hair-cut."

"Yes, signora," Enrico bowed, then turned and stalked off. Ellie noted that Lia and her step-grandson were not getting along as well as they had at first. Enrico's appearance was not her business, but he didn't seem as attractive to her now that she was in another place and Aldon was here.

They started out walking to the Denver Dry Goods, but Ellie went into the bank to cash the check her grandmother had sent for the wig.

That beautiful hair was a gold-mine for Ellie. She would thank her again for the gift of it. Grandmother was thrilled with the strength and thickness of the wig and postiches, and with Ellie's workmanship, too. She had surprised Ellie with a large amount of money, and Ellie knew the profit for the store would be good, as well. She could afford two dresses, new summer coat, a Stetson, a pair of boots, a long-sleeved tailored shirt, and trousers that would stand up to riding. She would also be able to pay for Aldon's new mirror.

After cashing the check, she waited for the light to change and crossed the street to the Denver Dry Goods Company. In the elevator, she watched the numbers climb. When it stopped with a *ding* the operator slid the door open and Ellie emerged into the ladies department. When she heard Lia's voice shouting, she knew where to go. She saw three clerks in long-sleeved black dresses rushing back and forth with piles of chiffon and taffeta over their arms before she saw Lia. One of the clerks nodded in the direction of the voice which was coming from a dressing room.

"Go to the men's department," Lia commanded when Ellie stuck her head through the curtain. "See to Enrico. He is such a child! The suit will have to be measured perfect because it will come in the mail barely in time for the parties and there will be no time to send it back so they can alternate it."

Ellie went downstairs where Enrico postured while a tailor tried to wrap a measuring tape around his waist. She decided to wait a few moments before she approached the two men.

For the rest of her time in the men's department, Ellie nodded or shook her head over the clothes and accessories offered to Enrico. He tried on a black suit and the hat he wanted. He and Ellie then went to find Lia who, when she heard them talking, stuck her head between the curtains and commanded, "Enrico, you sit over there in the slipper chair and Ellie you come in here with me. I have selected a few things for you to try."

When Ellie saw the pale green-gold frock with gold embroidery on the wide belt, she threw off her skirt and blouse and tried it on over her chemise. It flowed over her slender body as if cut and fashioned just for her.

"You will wear this one to Molly's birthday," said, Lia. "And here is mine," she picked up a rose, silk dress with tiers of ruffles that fell to mid-ankle. "And now let us buy something for Molly's birthday."

They shopped for Molly then bought casual clothes for themselves. When they stepped into the lunch room each wore something new.

CHAPTER 25

ELLIE

At lunch time, Ellie, Lia and Enrico followed a haughty waiter to a table in the hotel dining room. They ordered chicken cordon bleu, which was delivered to their table accompanied by fresh, tender green beans and scalloped potatoes. After a baked Alaska for dessert, Lia persuaded Ellie to go with her to a shoe store she'd seen on the way there. They left Enrico with enough money to pay the bill and arranged to meet him later at the hotel.

Lia wanted to look at every shoe in the downtown area. Although they found the perfect footwear to match their ensembles, Ellie wanted nothing more than to go back to the hotel. If she had wanted to spend her time in stores, she might as well have stayed in Chicago.

When Ellie eventually got to her room, she lay down on the bed and fell into a deep sleep. An hour later, she woke up feeling groggy, and knowing she'd heard a car horn. Looking at the sidewalk through the window, she saw the top of a long, black automobile at the curb. A man in a Stetson got out and he had not taken two steps when she recognized him. He looked and waved her down. Although her granddad had taught her to wait for a gentleman to knock on the door, she shelved the rule, threw on, her new, green tea-dress, grabbed her light, cream jacket, and ran down the stairs.

In the lobby, she looked around for Aldon and saw him in one of the glass compartments in the revolving door. He paused to let a woman in another enclosure step out then motioned Ellie to step into his with him. Standing close they synchronized the movement of their feet, but before Ellie had time to get in step, Aldon had somehow wafted her onto the sidewalk. He took her hand and she had to run to keep up as he made for the automobile.

As they pulled away, Ellie realized she hadn't told Lia where she was going. She pulled back her shoulders and sat up straight. She had tended to Lia's needs and desires for months, and now, she decided, she would tend to Ellie's for a while.

Once the sun went down, the heat of the day passed quickly. She rolled up the windows on her side, and Aldon rolled his up too.

"Cold? Come sit close to me. My brothers always said I give off as much heat as a pot-bellied stove.

As she moved closer, she recalled how standoffish she had felt when they first met and yet how she had availed herself of his warmth even as she tried to be prim and proper. Now, he laid his hand palm up on the seat between them and she put hers into it.

"Let the lower lights be burning," Aldon began a chorus in his light tenor, and the joy in Ellie's heart reached a new level. "Send a gleam across the wave." They had sung that one in church with Pastor Rudd several times, and she loved it. "Some poor fainting, struggling seaman you may rescue, you may save." As the sun sank behind the mountains and the stars began to twinkle, Ellie and Aldon approached the foothills

When the road began to rise, he let go of her hand to maneuver the next curve. That was when Ellie saw the roadhouse with smoke rising from its chimney. Aldon parked came to open the car door for her. Her mouth watered when she smelled the well-seasoned meal that must be waiting for them.

"This is the, "Oklahoma Inn." It's run by one of my war buddies. I think you'll like him. It's the only commercial place where you can get real barbecue and it's so good I'd eat it every day if I could."

The door opened to a blast of noise and heat. A cowboy band played, California Here I Come." The room felt cozy with the odor of bathed bodies, Evening in Paris perfume, and hair pomade. She smelled the pine that had been carpentered into walls and booths. A tall man in a red-sauce stained apron set down a pair of tongs and came to wait on them. Aldon jumped up to shake his hand, then the two men slapped each other on the back, a semi-violent rite that still seemed strange to Ellie. She saw, though, that the two of them were simply hiding their liking for each other under a manly reserve.

"This here's my buddy, "Oklahoma," Aldon said.

"How do you do?" Ellie stuck out her hand to shake the huge paw shoved toward her.

"How-do, ma'am. Welcome to, "Oklahoma Inn. I'm Oklahoma.""

"It's his nickname. He was a code-talker during the war." Aldon said. The big man grinned when he saw the puzzled look in Ellie's eyes.

"I'm half Choctaw, half white. I lived with the Indians first, then some white people took me to raise, so I learned both languages. When my Choctaw brother went to war, I went too. All we did was tell secrets in our own language. The Huns were flummoxed. My buddy here," he slapped Aldon on the back, recommended I come to Denver for a job and I got on here. Eventually saved up enough to buy the place. He motioned for Ellie to sit down and then sat next to her his bulk squashing her against the wall.

Ellie had believed that American Indians were stoical and close-mouthed, but Oklahoma nodded and smiled and went on talking. "That Aldon, he's a fine man. We weren't in the same division, but when we found out how much we both liked horses we got to be real good friends. Nice meetin' you ma'am. Sorry I got to get back to work now. He got up and walked away. "

When they finished the meal, Aldon stood and held out his arms inviting Ellie to dance. Hoping the evening would never end, she tried to concentrate as he led her in the two-step to the tune of, "Don't Fence Me in," to a lively beat.

CHAPTER 26

ELLIE

"We'd better get back to town, somebody will be missing us," Aldon said when they'd been dancing for a while. He twirled Ellie out and then brought her back into his arms. Taking her hand, he walked her over to the register where he paid the bill. They stopped at the table to leave a tip for the waitress. Once they were in the car, Aldon pressed the electric starter and the engine responded immediately. They looked at each other and grinned.

"No more cranking," Aldon said.

"This car's got the moxy." Ellie felt giddy and carefree as they picked up speed curving down the mountain road. When Aldon shifted into second gear to slow the car, Ellie clapped.

"Saves the brakes," Aldon looked over at her and nodded. As they left the mountains behind, the road leveled out and he shifted into third gear. Back at the hotel, they discovered that Lia and Enrico were missing, then Ellie remembered Lia's plan to visit the Tuileries Amusement Park.

"We might as well go on over there," Aldon said. "We can give them a ride back to the hotel."

As they approached the park, Ellie gazed at a halo of light beaming from the permanent fairground. She wound down the side window the better to hear the faraway throbbing of a drum. The Ferris wheel, its

99

lights gleaming, rotated against the night sky. Terrified, but delighted screams flew into the night air as a string of roller-coaster cars steamed up one loop and roared down the next.

After parking, they walked into a thin cloud of dust and the smell of cotton candy. When they came to a shooting gallery, Ellie felt her confidence rise. Now was the time to show Aldon that the lessons he'd given her in spare bits of time had made her into a sharp shooter.

"Step right up! Three shots for a nickel," the man behind the counter shouted. Aldon gave him a coin and the two of them started competing for points. They only grew tired of the game when it became obvious that their scores would forever match. Ellie laid down her rifle and the booth-tender started shoving stuffed animals into her arms.

"Well done," Aldon said, patting her on the back. He took some of the animals from her. "Won't Seraphina be surprised when we get home?" He placed a free arm around her waist. "Let's go put these in the car so we won't have to carry them around."

After they had deposited the toys, Ellie asked if they could go to the merry go round. She hadn't been on one since she was a child, but recalled it as a happy experience. Aldon bought tickets and they stepped onto the platform just as the carousel music began and the giant machine started to move. Ellie sat sidesaddle while Aldon straddled his horse, his feet firmly on the wooden floor which turned with the horses. The animals rose and fell pulling Ellie into a kind of dream as if she were being rocked in a cradle. Soon, tears ran down her cheeks, and yet she had no feeling of melancholy or sadness. The sound of the booming drum, the ragtime piano, and the majestic notes from the steam organ seeped into her body. She felt as if ice was melting inside her. When the merry-go- round came to a rest, Aldon helped her down, and steered her to a bench. He gave her a big, white handkerchief and sat down next to her, putting his arm around her shoulders.

"Why are you crying?" he asked when the emotional storm quieted.

"I don't know. I don't think there's anything wrong with me. In fact, I haven't felt this happy since I was a child. Isn't that strange?" She looked up into his face searching for an answer.

CHAPTER 27

ELLIE

Over Aldon's shoulder, Ellie saw the Ferris wheel slow to a stop. She then noticed someone in a gondola waving and calling.

"It's getting late and the Signora is probably wondering how to get a taxi back to the hotel." Aldon said.

"The Signora, is right over there." Ellie said staring across the fairway.

"Hoo, hoo." Their employer waved. When they had walked the few paces to the wheel, she shouted, "Where have you been? I have lost Enrico!"

"Are you all right?" Forgetting her own former emotional state, Ellie lifted the bar over Lia's lap and gave her a hand. "

"Am I all right?" Lia said shaking Ellie off. "You left me without a fare-thee-well, and now Enrico has disappeared. No, I am notta all right. We must find him so we can go back to the hotel."

"I'll get him." Aldon strode away, and the women hurried after him. Lia chattered loudly as they went and people kept looking back and staring.

"Really, that Enrico, he is too bad. He has no self-discipline. He is always going to the saloon in town, I give him money and money and he always needs more. He comes home broken every night." In the garish carnival lights, Lia stopped and rubbed her fingers together in Ellie's face. It was the ancient sign for money.

"You mean broke?" Ellie asked, imagining how the local people would say it.

"Yes, n-ever no m-oney and in his chips, as well." In her anger Lia stammered.

"In his cups, you mean…drunk?"

"Drunk, yes. I will tell my Giovanni he must send his grandson to Switzerland, or Italy, or wherever he wants to go. I want my peace back. I want my home again."

As the crowd thinned on the outskirts of the amusement park, they saw Aldon cut between two tents toward the sound of men's loud voices. When Ellie and Lia got to the small alleyway, they saw Enrico slumped against a tent post like a rag doll. A man came at Aldon, but Lia, in her hurry to get to Enrico, rushed past and the man accidently knocked her down. Ellie hurried to help, but Lia was getting to her feet unharmed.

"Stop this nonsense at once," Ellie cried. When Aldon heard her voice, it took his mind off protecting himself, and a punch landed on his jaw. One of the men ran over to search through Enrico's pockets. He pulled out a roll of bills and shoved them in his pocket, and the three of them took off running.

Ellie ran back to the fairway, and almost collided with a policeman waving a night stick, who must have heard about the fight. He pulled back to hit Aldon but Ellie grabbed his arm and held on as hard as she could. The man hesitated.

"Not him," Ellie said, trembling. "The bad guys are gone. See if that other man is all right."

"A word to the wise," the policeman said trying to get Enrico to his feet, "Take this man home and don't bring him back to town again. If I ever see any of you again, I'll arrest you all."

Aldon took Enrico from the policeman and Ellie put her hand under the young man's elbow to help support him. Lia followed them to the Packard Six, and Aldon stuffed Enrico into the back seat. He shoved him over, and got in.

"You'll have to drive," Aldon told Ellie. "I'm still woozy from that punch. We leave for the valley at six o'clock in the morning."

CHAPTER 28

ELLIE

Molly's birthday came two days after they arrived at home, and when Ellie took Lia's breakfast up Lia told her to ask Molly to come up, too.

"Lia requests the pleasure of your company in her suite." Ellie told Molly at the kitchen sink.

"*Suite* is it?" Molly placed her hands on her hips and stood staring at Ellie as if she were a stranger.

"Please, she wants to be friends." Ellie tented her hands under her chin in a pleading gesture.

"Humph, it'll be the first time that besom ever thought about anybody but herself." Molly stalked down the hallway and up the staircase leaving Ellie five paces behind. "What do you want now," she said as soon as Lia came to the door. Lia took her hand and led her over to the bed where a complete set of garments lay spread on the coverlet.

"Look what we bought you in Denver; will you try them on?" Lia lifted the dress and held it against herself.

"My stars, and garters," Molly said. "Is all that for me? But why?"

"Isn't it pretty? It's the right color for your redheaded complexion." Lia held the dress out toward Molly.

"I ain't been a redhead in a long time," the housekeeper said, taking the dress and stroking its blue-violet voile. "My, it is fine and soft."

Lia moved behind the housekeeper and pulled one of her apron strings, Molly dropped the dress on the bed, grabbed her apron, and hung on. "You two go on in the other room. I've never had anyone watch me dress and I'm not starting now."

On the way past the Victrola, Lia paused to put on a record and wind the machine which emitted lively ragtime jazz.

"Do you think Molly ever wore rayon stockings?" Lia said, prancing to the music. "We'll have to check whether she got her seams straight."

"I wonder if she has ever worn a silk chemise before," Ellie said dancing too. "Just think, this is only the first stage of the surprises."

They heard a lady-like cough and looked up to see Molly standing in the doorway chin up and shoulders back looking like a photograph of royalty on the front page of The Denver Post.

"You look beautiful," Ellie said. "Do you like your present?"

"Oh, yes. I'll wear this outfit for Sunday-go-to-meetings for the rest of my life: in the summer that is." Molly said. Lia walked her to the cheval mirror in the corner.

"Why I'm just a regular Miss Got-Rocks, ain't I?" Molly turned her head one way and then another admiring herself. "Why did you do all this, anyhow?"

"Happy birthday, dear Molly," said Lia giving her a careful hug.

"How did you know?" Molly turned to Ellie

"A little bird told us," she said.

"Most likely Aldon," Molly nodded. "Well, ain't that just like him? I'm going to get out of this garb and back into my housedress so I can start supper."

"Lets' go down and wait for the men to come in so they can see the new Molly first," said Lia.

It took some persuasion, but Molly consented to being shown off with the stipulation that she could, "get comfortable" as soon as she had been adequately admired by the fellows. Ellie and Lia escorted her to the parlor, then went back upstairs to change into their new dresses.

Back in the kitchen, Molly wore a clean apron over her dress. Pots and pans rattled. Suspicious, she set her head at an angle and stared at younger women.

"Why are you dressed up?" she said. At that moment, Aldon and Signor Solano entered the room

"Bella, bella," the Signor said looking from one to the other.

"Molly, you look so fine," Aldon said. "Wait until…"

"Where is my grandson?" Signor Solano interrupted.

"Let's go for a ride," said Aldon. "He's probably going to meet up with us later."

"But what about supper?" Molly asked.

"We have time." Aldon guided her out the back door and to the Solano's touring car, which Ellie would drive. He joined Kate and Seraphina in his flivver.

When Colleen met them at the door of the hotel, she raved over Molly's new dress and asked her to follow her into the dining room. Two women rose from their seats and came to Molly who swayed slightly when she saw them.

"Nancy!" she said, hugging the tall, willowy one. She then turned to the other, "Trudy!

Aldon took Ellie over to the small group and introduced her, first to his mother, Nancy, then to his aunt, Gertrude.

"How do you do?" said Nancy. "I have heard about you coming all the way from Chicago to work on the ranch. How are you liking it?"

"It's the prettiest place I've ever seen," said Ellie, noticing the resemblance between the tall, thin Aldon and his mother.

"Aunt Gertrude," said Aldon, eyes twinkling, this is Ellie, our *hired hand.*" Gertrude who was shorter and rounder grabbed Ellie in a hug and almost suffocated her.

Colleen gave suggestions for seating as Kenny came in. The room sounded like an aviary full of birds chirping as they looked forward to being fed.

"This is your birthday celebration, Aunt Molly. We wanted to surprise you." Aldon said.

"Faith and begorra," said Molly. I never thought anything like this would happen to me, and me having done nothing to deserve it."

CHAPTER 29

ELLIE

That evening Ellie ate the best steak she had ever had. The devil's food cake would make her memory salivate for years to come. She didn't know what to do about the appetite she had developed, if she didn't watch it, she'd be ten pounds heavier when she left here.

When dinner was over, Molly got up to stack dishes, but Colleen came in and stopped her. "You go on, Molly, this is the only chance you've had in your life not to wash dishes. Happy birthday, my dear friend."

One by one each of the guests hugged Molly. After his turn, Aldon said to the waiting group, "Let's take a walk." They all went out the front door and onto the sidewalk: Signor and Signora Solano, Nancy and Gertrude, Kate and Seraphina, Ellie and Aldon. The group threaded their way through the strolling ranchers and their families who all seemed drawn toward the same place, a flashing theatre marquee where the words, "The Thief of Bagdad" shone in neon brightness."

"Wait, boy! Where you going?" Molly pulled back, but Aldon tugged her arm so that she was impelled to go along. They walked into the theater lobby, which was only a small room decorated in red velvet.

Molly stared open mouthed as though she had never seen anything so elegant.

"Popcorn, Molly?" Mr. Fitz asked from behind the wooden counter. The aroma as the white kernels popped and fell into a snowy heap against the glass gave Ellie's taste-buds something else to long for. Mr. Fitz filled the bags and passed them to her and she gave one to each person in the party. Seraphina didn't want to share so Mr. Fitz filled another bag for her. When Aldon tried to put the nickels into his hand, the grey-haired gentleman waved him away. "On the house," he said.

"Where's Ellie," Molly asked.

"Here I am." Ellie slipped into place, following the herd into the theater. When they entered and filed into seats, Kenny played a fanfare on the upright piano at the foot of the stage. On stage, Colleen stepped in front of the curtain and stood waiting for the theater to quiet.

"Ladies and gentlemen, please join us in singing, "*Happy Birthday*", to Molly," she said

In the dimly lit theater, everyone heard Molly say tearfully, "You mean…they're all going to sing for me?"

"Yes, dear lady," said Signor Solano. "Would you like to sit down and enjoy your birthday song?

When the song ended and everyone else took their seats, someone from the back yelled, "Take off your hats!" Women's bob-hats and old-fashioned, wide-brimmed chapeaus vanished into laps. A hush fell over the audience, and a "Felix the Cat," cartoon began.

Seraphina reached for Ellie and Ellie took her on her lap. The small child giggled and laughed, but by the time, "The Thief of Bagdad," came on she was asleep held safe in Ellie's arms.

When the movie ended, Aldon picked Seraphina up and carried her out to the street where they dispersed to go to their separate motors. Nancy and Trudy had come up from Artesia in a coup which had a rumble seat no one wanted to ride in. Later when Ellie asked Molly what she liked best about the movie, the housekeeper said that everything was too wonderful to be able to choose. When Lia insisted on an answer, Molly confessed that Kenny's music had enhanced the excitement to the point where she chewed her fingernails down to the quick. Soon, though, their own brilliant young musician played such soothing music that she knew the lovers would be safe. She cried with relief as they flew over onion domes, spires, and pillars, and left the air above the exotic city for the clean, pure atmosphere of the desert and mountains.

"Indeed, that was a lovely show, thank you all." Molly said.

CHAPTER 30

ELLIE

Wham, bang, crash! Ellie awoke with a start. Someone was making a ruckus in the house. She slid out of bed, dressed, and stepped carefully down the stairs avoiding the creaky boards discovered from morning trysts with Aldon. From the kitchen, she heard a rough, country voice." Git the booze if you know what's good for you."

"Si, si, but should we not hide from the bad men? They followed us from town and will arrive soon." It was Enrico's voice. She heard the basement door open and the sound of feet pounding down the stairs.

Ellie knew she must get to Aldon. She opened the front door and slipped out into the misty night. Before she could reach the barn, she heard another commotion and ran behind the chicken coop to hide. A soft, *no* escaped her lips when she peeked out and saw men in masks getting out of a motor car. They lit torches, which flared orange in the darkness. She knew they couldn't see her so she ran into the barn and clambered up the ladder to the loft.

"Aldon!" she hissed standing over his cot. "Wake up!"

He turned on his side facing her and pulled her onto the cot beside him. He put his arms around her and snuggled back into sleep.

"Aldon, get up. We've got visitors," Ellie pushed against his chest and he abruptly let go. She fell onto the floor and lay there a moment getting her breath back.

"Come on, there's something happening out there. We're being attacked." She rose and shook his shoulder.

He sprang up. "Get that shotgun over there,"

She handed him the weapon in the corner as he grabbed two shells from a drawer in the desk and loaded both barrels.

"Stay here," he said.

"Wait, let me tell you." She tried for a deep breath but felt so rushed she couldn't quite manage it. "Enrico's in the basement going after some liquor. Two more men are waiting for him in the kitchen. I think they're drunk. Some guys in masks just arrived – four of them in an open flivver. They're in the barnyard, wearing robes and hoods, and they have torches. We'll have to be careful they don't burn down the barn."

"Okay, you've done a good job, now you stay right here where you'll be safe and let me handle it."

"I'm going," she said. "Just tell me what to do."

"We don't have time to argue about it." He said descending the ladder.

"I'll show myself and divert their attention and you can get a drop on them." She scrambled after him, brushed past, and ran out the door before he could forbid it. She screamed to get the marauders' attention, and they turned and stared.

"Get her," one of them yelled.

"Put those torches in the air and hold them high. Okay, now, know this. I'm going to shoot the first man that moves." Aldon stepped out of the shadows pointing the gun. "Ellie come over here by me."

"It's a mite late to go visiting, isn't it?" Aldon said. "Keep your hands in the air and go stand over there in front of the corral."

"We hear you're harboring some folk that don't belong here." One of the men said.

"Where did you hear that?" Aldon walked toward the men.

"From that there Eyetalian you got hanging around here. He don't belong neither, but he sure is a poor poker player." The men laughed.

"Who are you after?" asked Aldon.

"For now we want that colored woman. Her husband was a

murderer. What better reason could we have for taking her away?" Another man spoke.

"You're not taking anybody away from here. Head back down the mountain. You're the ones who don't belong." Aldon made a shooing motion with the gun barrel.

"You see, you don't understand. We are here to protect you and your family from foreigners and strangers coming in and taking over." A man with a big belly spoke.

"First off, they got to be white." The clansman's torch rose when Aldon pointed the gun at him.

"Not just them, but their folks too." They seemed to talk in turn, one and then the other as if the spiel were rehearsed. "They got to have American names, American ways, fight for the country."

"Did you fight for the country?" Aldon asked while Ellie gave a sigh of impatience.

"We're all respectable businessmen and upstanding citizens, some-body had to stay here and run the country. Our leader is the preacher of the biggest church in Artesia. He's a real American. We got half the politicians in the state on our side. We're doing what any red-blooded Americans ought to be doing."

"We hear you've got a half-breed kid here, too," said a different voice. "We could take her off your hands."

Everybody jumped when the screen door banged shut and Kate came striding out in a long robe carrying the biggest broom Ellie had ever seen. She walked straight up to the fat man, and took a swing at him. He went down. She went after a second, and he ran, tripping over his feet.

"Get out of here and leave us alone." She turned on the third one who stared at her dumbfounded. She hit the fourth man with the broom. In three seconds the automobile was loaded and pulling away. Instead of watching it go, Kate looked around for someone else to hit and headed for Aldon, not quite recognizing him in the dark. He grabbed the broom.

"Whoa there, it's me. You've taken care of them. You can relax now."

Once Enrico and his two cohorts saw that the men in the robes had moved on, they came skulking out the back door. One of the men was tall and skinny. The other was broad and hairy. By now, Signor Solano had also descended from his aerie.

"What are these men doing here?" Signor Solano asked moving close to Enrico.

"Allow me to introduce my friends," said Enrico bowing to the company in a drunken move to take control of the situation.

"What are they doing here?" Signor Solano asked again while supporting his grandson against his own increasing strength.

"I know them," said Aldon. "They're squatters."

CHAPTER 31

ELLIE

When rodeo day came, Ellie put on the divided doeskin skirt, and fringed jacket Nancy had worn as rodeo queen. The outfit was of the softest leather Ellie had ever felt and she knew it would blend with Susie Q's and Sunrise's palomino coats. For a blouse, she wore a plaid taffeta shirtwaist with a high collar, in red and gold Molly found in the attic. Aldon told her she looked like she'd be rodeo queen next year if she stayed around. It could be a possibility, she thought if Aldon wanted her to. They outfitted the horses in hand-tooled tack made by Aldon's grandfather over fifty years ago. It gave Ellie a warm glow to think how much respect and love creations from the past could generate, and how useful they could still be. The final touch was Ellie's brown Stetson for which she had spent a great deal of money. She knew it would last her a lifetime, but she didn't know how long she would be in a place where she could wear it without looking strange. Stetsons for women certainly were not the rage in Chicago.

Aldon had saddled Susie Q and Chief and brought them to the back door. Sunrise would follow where his mother led. She mounted and Aldon got on Chief.

The day of the rodeo was clear with puffy clouds. As Aldon and Ellie went along the gravel road to town, they began to sing the songs they had rehearsed for Sunday Meeting the next day. When they spotted the spires of the churches, they sang, "When it's Springtime in the Rockies," and "Home on the Range." Having traveled the road so frequently on their way to town and back, by now each had memorized most of the songs the other knew. They sang: cowboy songs, hymns and some German songs. Ellie had taught Aldon a few classical ones she knew and he liked them so much he kept asking for more.

As they got closer to town horses and wagons gathered behind and in front of them. Everyone in the valley loved rodeo. Aldon's cousins came from their ranches in flivvers, in spring wagons, and on horseback. Everyone who would be in the parade clustered under the cottonwood trees near the creek at the Community Church. Cousins from the German band piled out of a huge wagon pulled by a matched pair of black and white Friesians with huge hooves and broad backs. The men wore their lederhosen and alpine caps. They were a strange enough sight, but when they started warming up, Sunrise got spooked and ran.

"He'll be back. It's the tubas." Aldon said. "My family always has too many tubas. Most of the instruments came from Prussia where, before the war, they made some of the best instruments in the world. You can look in any attic in the valley and there will be a tuba. The family almost disowned me when I chose the mandolin. One of these days, though, if I have enough wind left in me, I'll get down the Tuba and play it, too."

The parade-master walked among the crowd, trying to stay out of the way of the horses' feet. He spoke to each group, telling them where they belonged in the line-up. The clowns with their brooms and shovels were assigned groups of horses to follow and clean up after. The Artesia school band had come to march too. There was no high-school in the area so that the students who wished to go on must board in town. Few did as no one seemed to see a need for a high-school diploma when they had so much practical and hard-earned experience with ranching.

Susie Q was almost prancing when she and Chief passed the family on the sidelines. Seraphina jumped up and down and waved her arms. "Ellie, Aldon!" she yelled. Kate tried to quiet her, but the little girl was too excited to calm down.

CHAPTER 32

ALDON

Dear Bill,

After the parade with all the rousing music and the prancing horses, we riders stood under the cottonwood trees near the church, so the people could come up and say hello. Chief showed that he had adopted Susie Q and Sunrise by biting at any horses that came near him. His teeth came within an inch of Dieter's horse, but Dieter kicked at him and he backed off.

It seems we've done nothing but practice for the grand entry, which is my favorite part of the rodeo. This was the best rodeo because Ellie was there for all the practices. She carried the Colorado flag. We had a stiff wind and it was hard for her to hold onto it even though she had the pole in the stirrup holster. She and Susie Q practically flew into the arena. The Spaetzli band played, the crowd cheered, and everyone stood to salute the American flag. The line peeled off into a four-leaf clover smooth as could be.

That's a good rodeo grounds. Remember when Dad took us along to build the grandstands and the corrals? Paul and I got into trouble because we played around too much, but you helped like the daddy's boy you were.

This year I won a cash prize for bull riding. Man, I got a devil of a bull. After the buzzer went he threw me and then tried to gore me.

Thank the Lord for Willy. Those clowns save so many lives, it isn't even funny. Ha.

Ellie couldn't figure out why a fellow would get on an animal that was never meant to be ridden, risk being stomped, and have to run for his life. She does have a point. I plan to have that be my last bull-ride. There are other things in life besides showing how tough you are by getting your bones smashed up. I was glad for the prize money, though. I don't want Signor Solano paying for all the ranch improvements.

Ellie told me earlier that she wanted to race Susie Q. I was sorry to inform her that no woman had ever raced on our track before, but when Nancy heard me explaining, she got all huffy and she and Gertrude took off to badger their brothers into letting Ellie race. They'll do about anything for Nancy so the next thing we knew Ellie was on the list.

When Enrico heard Ellie was racing he wanted to race too. Signor Solano asked me to give him the best horse we had, but that was Chief and I just couldn't do it. He rode Stardust, the next fastest. We didn't know how Susie Q would do, but I wasn't about to ask Ellie to loan her out. Enrico isn't any kind of rider, so he came in dead last, anyhow. It wouldn't have mattered whose horse he rode. Signor was so glad to see his boy interested in something he was satisfied. Chief got first place, Kenny's horse got second and Susie Q did well, for a first race, coming in third.

After the rodeo the Fitzgeralds opened the old hotel bathhouse so folks could take baths without going back to the ranches. The Fitz's still charge two-bits a bath, but they don't make much profit because they pay the employees to empty and fill tubs. You'll recall that some family members share the same water.

When Mrs. Fitz was ready to practice before the dance, the band went up to the hall over the general store. The cousins showed up with guitars, fiddles and drums, and Colleen played ragtime on the old Tonk piano while we tuned up.

A few of the women came to let us know they were ready for the fireworks out at the reservoir. That was another grand entry, but as far as I was concerned, Ellie was the only woman there. She had on this dress that was the green of the leaves when they first come out in spring. It had some kind of gold on it that matched her hair. I tell you brother, the sight of her would make a man weak in the knees.

The town council voted to spend a lot of money on pyrotechnics this year. About dusk, we workers went around to the other side of the dam to set off the spectacle. You won't believe this, Bill, but when we got all the fireworks, including spinning wheels and Roman Candles, laid out, the first display blew up and set off all the rest. Before we knew it, we had a shower of colored lights that illuminated the sky for miles around. They looked pretty reflecting in the lake for all of three minute, but then it all went up in smoke. The mayor was so furious he headed for his automobile saying he was going to the fireworks salesman in Artesia and knock his block off. We managed to talk him out of it, but he took his wife down to City Hall to typewrite a letter of complaint.

It didn't take long to get to the dance where they had the platform set up at the foot of the range. The folks enjoy the dance, but I never really cared about it. From the time we were boys, mother scrubbed us until our skin burned, then slicked back our hair with Madagascar oil. She parted it in the middle, remember that? We looked like little Lord Fauntleroys. We had to wear those suits, and above all, we had to behave like gentlemen. She took turns dancing with us when she wasn't making us play our instruments. We had to smile the whole time and it made our faces hurt. With Ellie there though, I was thankful for Nancy's determination to make gentlemen of us. Dad's too.

CHAPTER 33

ALDON

Brother, this is a long letter, but I thought I'd work on it when I had time then I could put it all in one envelope and save on postage.

I'll tell you about the dance. Once the band got going, the Solanos didn't miss a set, and every uncle and male cousin asked Ellie to join them on the floor. Believe me, she learned fast to keep her feet out of the way of their clodhoppers. Usually no man asks any woman to dance except his wife and sometimes his sister, but Ellie has a way about her that puts you at ease, and she's so daggone shiny, they couldn't help themselves. Dieter, then Arn went off the band stand to dance with her, so I did too. When I got right up to her I suddenly turned shy and didn't know what to say. I might have chickened out altogether, but she smiled and put her arms out to me and I was a goner.

The band started the Varsouviana and she shook her head saying, "I can't do this dance."

"All right." I turned away thinking she didn't want to dance with me, after all.

"Could you teach me, though?" she asked and my heart flipped over.

"Why sure! Here's how we start." We had a couple of laughs

wrestling to get the arms right. It came to me why people like to dance so much…so's they can hold each other. All that practice, just so you can put your arms around somebody, Mother never told us about that part. We wouldn't have liked it if she had. At first Ellie couldn't get the hang of it, so I showed her a few steps and sang those words the school-teacher (Ma) taught us: *put your little foot, put your little foot, put your little foot right down.*

"I hate to tell you, but what I'm seeing is *not* a little foot," she said, looking at my boots. I laughed so hard she finally had to slap me to make me shut up. Ha, not hard, just a tap on the cheek.

She soon got the hang of it and we rotated around the floor with all the other dancers. Throughout the evening, Nancy and Gertrude took turns with their three hefty brothers and with dad's brother, Ernest, who lost his wife last year.

I watched Signor Solano's grandson, Enrico, when he left the dance.

When you came back a couple of dances on, he bowed to Ellie like those foreigners do, but then he collapsed as if all the hot air had gone out of him. The band began to play again and the grandson struggled to his feet and pulled Ellie from her chair. That was when I laid my mandolin down and everybody got out of my way. It only took me three strides to get there. I grabbed the guy's collar in one hand and his belt in the other, drug him across the dance floor, and out to the flivver. I tossed him in for the second time. All the outside drinkers and the inside dancers came to watch what they hoped would be a fight. Too bad that man doesn't have any fight in him.

"What do you think you're doing?" Ellie was furious with *me!* "You didn't need to get rough with him, I could have handled it," she said.

"If you could, why didn't you?" I had to admire her spunk, but I knew which parts of how you act belong to the man and which belong to the woman. She didn't. I wished somebody had taught her to tend to the woman part and leave the man part to me.

"You didn't give me a chance. You knocked him out." She seemed disappointed in me and that was the worst thing of all.

"He passed out from drinking."

"Why did you have to go and make a scene?" Ellie lowered her voice. "What must your family think of me — a woman that men fight over?" We heard Enrico moan from the open car. She went peeked in.

"Ooh, Enrico, are you all right. I'm sorry Aldon did this to you. Are you hurt?" she was all mushy.

"I'll take him home," she said heading for the driver's door of my auto.

"You can't drive that."

"I can drive anything with wheels," she said. "I'm a woman, not some kind of hothouse flower. Get it through your thick skull that I can take care of myself. Up until now, Aldon, it has been a perfect day. I've never had a better one. It's too bad it had to end like this."

"Better that he passed out so he couldn't hurt you. You drive the Touring car." I told her. I slammed the door and got in. I drove away with Enrico bouncing around in the back.

CHAPTER 34

ELLIE

In her room that night, Ellie picked up the hog's-hair brush from her dressing table, yanked it through her hair one hundred times, and threw it back on the table. *Maybe I should go out to the barn and try to make Aldon understand how I feel,* she thought. She dug her fingers into a jar of cold cream and slathered it onto her face while she pictured herself telling Aldon off. *I can take care of myself. Don't you know that if people see men fighting over me, they'll think I'm a hussy? What business is it of yours who I dance with?*

She touched the corner of her eye and felt moisture but knew she wasn't crying. She had cream in her eye. She wiped it off with a towel, grabbed her nail file, and sawed away at the nail on the index finger of her right hand.

"May I come in?" Someone knocked gently on the frame of the open door. Glancing up, Ellie saw Aldon's mother, Nancy, smiling at her.

While trying to improve her countenance, Ellie invited Nancy to sit on the bed while she did the calisthenics she was taught in gymnasium at school.

As Nancy walked across, the floor her bedroom slippers made a soft padding sound on the linoleum. Ellie noticed that Aldon's mother was almost as tall as her son and that her hair was the same champagne color as his. A long braid hung down her back and a nimbus of curls framed her face, reminding Ellie of one of the Gish sisters in the moving pictures. Was it Dorothy or Lillian? She couldn't decide. Ellie's smile began to feel more genuine because Nancy had come to visit. She was, of course, still furious with Aldon, but now, Nancy's quiet spirit began to calm her.

"I admire you young girls. You take such good care of your figures. I hope you won't mind if I rest my back. I thought maybe we could talk while the house is quiet. I don't plan to stay long." She watched from the bed as Ellie jumped up and down flapping her arms. After she had done twenty-five jumping jacks, she touched her toes without bending her knees for the same number of times.

"This has been a long day," Ellie said, throwing herself on the bed next to Aldon's mother. She propped herself up on her elbow so she could look into Nancy's face.

"The boys slept in this room," Nancy said looking at the ceiling. "They had two beds, but like puppies in a nest, all piled into the same one. By the time they were seven, nine, and ten, they were horsing around so much that we gave each of them his own room. It didn't do any good, though. Every night, Paul and Bill sneaked into bed with Aldon as soon as he fell asleep, which was immediately."

"You really love your boys, don't you?" Ellie lay back on the pillow.

"Aldon was always their hero, especially Paul's." Nancy paused and Ellie knew she was thinking about the son that had not returned from the war. If only Ellie could load him into her ambulance and bring him back. But, in war days, bringing anyone back for a complete cure was rare. It was so sad, but many of the lads had already died by the time the medics arrived on the battle field.

"Aldon blames himself for setting an example by enlisting." Nancy seemed transfixed by the light bulb above the bed. "It's not Aldon's fault, Paul would have gone anyway, if only to prove to himself he wasn't a coward." Nancy spoke without emotion as if her grief had become a dull, but familiar ache. "It was always one of his dreams to become a soldier."

"But Bill didn't go to war." Ellie said.

"No, they thought he had a heart murmur, so they classified him 4-

F. We had no idea, except that he never had the stamina the others had. He was built small and never gained weight; which made him an excellent jockey. After the army rejected him he received quite a few white feathers in the mail. That made him feel so bad.

"What did he do about that?" Ellie asked.

"He's still trying to show himself and everybody else that he's got moxie." Nancy smiled as if proud of her modern language. In his letters he says he takes on the most daring stunts," Nancy answered.

"Lots of boys and men had heart conditions and other problems too," said Ellie.

"Not one of my boys was ever afraid of anything, though," Nancy continued. "Paul was a daredevil. He decided one day that he and his brothers would play a game they called *Icarus*. Bill jumped off the barn first, but he wasn't' hurt, neither was Aldon, but Paul broke his leg and was on crutches for weeks."

"I hate for any man to have to go to war." Ellie said, covering a yawn. The mattress felt just right, and she liked hearing about Aldon and his brothers even though in some parts it was heartbreaking.

"We gals sometimes don't understand the things men have to do." Nancy's voice grew softer. "They are willing to fight for their country and we're grateful for that."

"I don't understand any man except my granddad," Ellie said.

"Tell me about your family," Nancy raised up to fluff her pillow then lay back down again. "Your opa makes his living from cattle too?"

"Not now, first he was a miner, then he became a cattleman. After that, he and Grandmother bought a dry-goods store." Sudden gratitude for Nancy's gentle company filled Ellie, but she reminded herself that she still had reason to resent the lovely woman's son.

CHAPTER 35

ELLIE

"Where were you born? " Ellie sat with her back against the head of the bed while Nancy lay flat.

"My people came from Germany in 1876 and built a cabin first thing." said Nancy.

"My mother and her sister were born here in Colorado, they lived in a cabin, too, but the stork dropped me in Chicago." Ellie settled in for a short chat with Aldon's mother. "Was Trudy your only sister?" Ellie wanted to know about Aldon's family whether she stayed at the ranch or not. It would be something to think about when she was alone.

"Yes, Trudy was the eldest. After me, Papa got what the ranch needed, which was a passel of boys."

"How many is a passel?" Amazed at how much better she felt talking to Nancy, Ellie began to relax.

"For us it was four. Karl died of the Spanish Influenza in 1918." Nancy's voice faltered.

"I'm so sorry. Your brothers are quite the gentlemen. I danced with them, you know." Ellie smiled to herself thinking of the gallant older men who each in his own way reminded her of a giant."

"Those big old fellows are as easy-going as they come, but they've had a great deal of hardship in their lives. They told me you were a sweet little thing. You received their blessing." Nancy said.

"A sweet little thing?" Ellie sat up fully awake staring at Nancy. "That's not how I want to be thought of."

"Oh, no? How do you want them to think of you?" Nancy touched Ellie's elbow as if to console her.

"As a good, strong, capable woman like you." Ellie felt the anger simmering again as she recalled Aldon's embarrassing and unnecessary rescue.

"You *are* strong and capable." Nancy reached up and laid her warm hand against Ellie's cheek. "And beautiful, too, no wonder Aldon is enraptured by you."

"He's what?" Ellie jerked her head back.

"Are you attracted to him? "Nancy asked.

"Well, I was, but..."

"His temper worries you." Nancy nodded.

"I don't like the idea of men fighting over me. That doesn't do a woman's reputation any good, does it?" Ellie started to get up, but when her feet hit the cold floor, she changed her mind. Ready now to talk in earnest she rested her back against a pillow and the iron rungs of the bedstead.

"I have never seen him jealous before. Maybe he's going to have to learn not to be, but he has always been protective and that will stay with him." Nancy pulled herself into a sitting position like Ellie's.

"He hasn't said much about his father," Ellie glanced at Nancy to gauge her expression in reaction to the question.

"Robert had a rough upbringing, but he was a good man. He believed in discipline for children and horses, all our people did."

"When did you know you loved Robert?" Ellie asked. Both pair of legs stretched toward the foot of the bed and Ellie pulled up the quilt.

"Being neighbors, our families worked the ranches together. On joint workdays, Robert kept my brothers from teasing me too much. They had a lot of respect for him. At haying time one year, when I was about eight, I was wearing a blue-print flour sack dress and running in the meadow with my hair flying. Robert caught me up under the arms and turned in circles with me. It made me dizzy, but when he set me down, he said I was as pretty as a Mountain Bluebird. It always makes me happy to think about that time. Eleven-year-old boys don't usually speak kindly to small girls let alone protect them from their brothers. I knew he must have thought a lot of me to call me after a Mountain Bluebird. They are one of the prettiest things you ever saw." She sighed. "They get their color from the sky."

"Robert was small and dark-headed. Men sometimes called him Shorty and sometimes Pee Wee. He always resented it, but once he proved he was a fighter, they stopped. When I got my growth, I was taller than he was, and when we started stepping out we took some teasing. Inside, though, he was the biggest man I ever knew."

"What happened to your Robert?" Ellie scooted down in the bed taking her pillow with her.

"After the war — after Paul..." Nancy sighed and drew her knees up under the cover with a low moan. "He got so sad he'd barely speak. It broke my heart, and I tried everything to cheer him. I grieved for Paul, too, but I knew I would see him again. It was awful to lose my husband to bitterness, but I still had two that needed me.

"When you lose your best friend and want to tell somebody about it, it would be your best friend whom you would tell, and it's the loneliest feeling in the world." Ellie wondered if that made sense as she closed her eyes for a moment. Biting her lower lip, she willed herself not to cry.

"You're right, Robert always did his work, but he couldn't find any peace, so he took to sitting at the kitchen table late into the night drinking beer. At first, I tried to stay and visit, but I couldn't stay awake all night and do chores the next day, so I started coming upstairs without him. One morning in the wee hours, I realized he hadn't come to bed, so I went downstairs and he was still at the table. I thought he had just laid his head down, but when I touched him, I knew he was gone." Nancy dabbed at her eyes with the sheet.

CHAPTER 36

ELLIE

Nancy's voice had become full of pauses and sighs. She sounded so burdened with the memory of her husband's death that Ellie didn't know what to do or say.

"Aldon was still gone, Bill had left for California, so I woke Molly who was living with us, and she saddled Ribbons and rode for help. While she was gone, I sat with Robert and said goodbye. My brothers came and built a coffin from lumber we had for the barn. Molly and I washed him and dressed him in clean clothes. We buried him on the ridge in the spot where he liked to sit on his horse and look out over the valley."

"You just buried him, you didn't have a coroner or an undertaker? There was no death certificate?" Having come from a large city Ellie had never heard of folks dealing with their dead in this way.

"We've never even had a doctor. Few communities do even now." Nancy fingered a quilt knot.

"Did Aldon come home then?"

"The war was over, and they let him muster out. He was so war-weary I wondered if he'd ever get over it. He'd lost Paul and many of his young friends and now his father was gone. He did the outside work, and Molly and I helped while keeping up the cooking, laundry, and house work. You can't let things go or they'll get into such a mess that you'll never straightened them out. We raised whatever vegetables we could. Several years later, Trudy asked me to live with her in town because her husband had died and she was lonely. It was okay with Bill and Aldon. Aldon leased the ranch to the Solanos, and Bill headed west. Molly stayed on enjoying the excitement of the foreigners when they came." She smiled when she mentioned Molly and Ellie wondered whether she was thinking about the wonderful time they'd had taking Molly to dinner and the moving picture show.

The next thing Ellie was aware of was light streaming through the lace curtains. Someone had spread another quilt over the bed and, oh, there was Nancy. When she realized she had missed coffee time with Aldon, regret caught her by the throat. She coughed lightly, which woke Nancy. Remembering the conversation from the night before, Ellie suddenly recalled her anger with Aldon.

"Good morning," said Nancy.

Ellie got out of bed so Nancy could come from her side which was against the wall.

"What's wrong?" Nancy asked.

"I'm still mad at Aldon." Ellie picked up the robe hanging over the desk chair.

"Last night was completely unlike him. He would have protected any girl, but I've never seen him so mad. Did my son fall in love?" Nancy began making the bed. "Maybe if you talk to him…" she said softly.

"We'd better get ready for church. Hopefully the chores got done without me. Aldon and I usually do the milking together, but I don't suppose he needs me. He could milk both cows in the time it takes me to get the stool under one of them." Ellie had never been so disheartened.

"Does Betsy still stick her foot in the pail?" Nancy's question followed Ellie's hint to talk about something else.

"I thought I was the only one she did that to. She got so good at tormenting me that Aldon traded milkers. Spot didn't like me either. Aldon is the one who has a way with animals." Ellie already felt a kinship with Nancy.

"He's a good man," said Aldon's mother.

"Yes, he is, but now that he's been fighting over me, I'm afraid I'll be considered a floozy by everyone in the valley. I understand they already thought I was a flapper. Now they'll think I've been leading Enrico and Aldon on," Ellie hated that her anger with Aldon was making her sharp with Nancy.

"Aldon will be sorry that you're angry with him, but he may not be sorry he dealt with the other young man as he did. Please talk to him my dear, he's never cared for a woman as he does for you. You're in love with him too aren't you? It's not always easy for a man and a woman to communicate. Wouldn't you be sorry if a quarrel kept you apart for the rest of your lives?"

Ellie, seeing the truth in what Nancy said, nodded thoughtfully, got up, and pulled the blue suit from its hanger in the trunk.

CHAPTER 37

ELLIE

It was almost the end of summer — round-up time when Ellie drove to the station to meet her mother and grandparents off the Chicago train. The mountains, as yet, had no snow on them, but she knew from the talk around the table that Aldon was planning to bring the cattle down this week in order to avoid bad weather for the trek.

That afternoon, when she hugged the members of her small family in their elegant department store suits, she felt tall — tall and protective. When Granddad removed his hat she saw him in a way she hadn't before. Was his hair always pure white? Had his shoulders drooped slightly since the last time she saw him? Mother looked as if she were Grandmother's sister instead of her daughter, and Grandmother had lost so much weight she looked like an emaciated ladles-department floor model. Had they changed or had she developed a more mature way of looking at them? She would need to watch and listen in order to understand whether they had problems now that they hadn't had before or whether they were the same as always and it was she who had changed.

At the ranch, everyone came out to welcome them and usher them inside. Ellie, Kate, and Seraphina had moved to the third floor so that the guests would only need to climb one set of stairs. Aldon lugged their Alexander Clark Co. Ltd. luggage to their rooms right away so they could change into more comfortable clothing.

It wasn't quite suppertime when they came downstairs so Molly asked Ellie and Aldon to show them around. At the corral, they stood and watched Sunrise leap and mince around Susie Q. Ellie's mother, Vera, laughed at the colt's feistiness, and thanked Aldon for giving the mustangs to Ellie.

"She's a good horse. Did she write about how well she and Susie Q placed in the rodeo race?" Aldon asked.

At bedtime, Vera came up to her room carrying a brown-paper wrapped package. She handed it to her daughter and Ellie tore it open.

"That's beautiful," she said, running her hand around the smooth silver frame. When she glanced into her reflection, however, her face looked drawn, and she had shadows under her eyes.

"Thank you, it's just right. I hope he'll accept it from me." Ellie said putting it on the desk.

"Why would he not?" Vera asked. "What's going on between you and that handsome young cowboy?" Vera sat on the bed, and patted the spot beside her. Ellie sat down too. These bedrooms were smaller than the one on the second floor and had even less space for a private visit.

"I don't think anything is going on between us. Not anymore," Ellie sighed.

"Are you fond of him?" Vera lifted Ellie's chin and turned her head so the young woman would look at her. Ellie nodded.

"Does he love you?" Vera's voice held a poignancy her daughter had rarely heard.

"I thought he did." Ellie wiped away a tear, hoping her mother hadn't noticed that she was crying.

"But you're afraid of something?" Vera seemed genuinely interested. Suddenly, Ellie realized that all her life she and her mother had been nearly strangers. Vera was only sixteen years older and they could have been friends, but something had kept them apart. She did know that Vera was always busy keeping house and entertaining for Grandmother while she was either away at school or working at the store. She would love to know something about her own father –

anything would do. She had made up stories and fantasies about a handsome young man, but no one had told her about him.

"Are you afraid Aldon will leave you as you believe your father left us?" Vera asked.

"Did you love my dad before he abandoned us?" Ellie sensed a possibility of finally learning what had happened between her parents.

"No," Vera said taking a deep breath. "I didn't know him very well?"

"You didn't know…him?" Ellie gasped. "How else could you have had a child…? Ellie stared at Vera who now refused to meet *her* eyes.

"You had the best possible father in your Granddad, why don't we leave it at that?"

"Because, I want to know, I've always wanted to know."

"Oh, Honey, I love you, isn't that enough?" Vera lightly touched Ellie's knee.

"I know you love me. You've shown it in many ways. I'm so grateful for the work you've done to take care of us all. Living with Grandmother and Granddad instead of getting out on your own couldn't have been easy. Even though we didn't have much time together, you kept me clean, you fed me, and you dressed me. I realize there were times when you wanted to talk and I was too busy, and I'm sorry. Please, Mother, tell me the whole story."

CHAPTER 38

ELLIE

"I don't think you will understand about your father, but you're right, it's time you knew." Vera lay down and took a deep breath in preparation for telling her story. "Dad was a miner from Wales, and mother was a farm girl he met and married on his way to Colorado. He wanted to prospect for gold in Rockridge, high up in the mountains. I was born there in 1864. We lived in such a spread-out community that a cabin could be a mile up the ridge from its neighbor. The town, which was down by the railroad, had seven buildings: an assay and claims office, a general store, a Chinese laundry, a general store, a hotel and two saloons."

Ellie snuggled close to her mother like a child being told a bedtime story.

"A handful of families with children lived in log cabins. We didn't have a school. Your grandmother, Hester, taught us to read, write, and cipher and that was all. From then on she taught us practical things like cooking, sewing, and raising chickens. For extra income until *Da* made his strike Ma worked at the hotel and we took in laundry. My sister and I made sandwiches from rabbit meat, venison, whatever *Da* found to help feed us. We then took them to sell when the train stopped at the station.

"We also learned to shovel snow in order to get into and out of the cabin. There were times," she mused, "when the drifts were up under the eaves and we were snowed in.

"When your grandmother hit on the idea of teaching us to crochet we started ordering yarn from the Sears and Roebuck catalog and making afghans, sweaters, doilies, antimacassars and even doll clothes for a department store in Denver.

One day after I turned sixteen, Sis and I went down to the station with some grub. A fine gentleman got off the train. I'd never seen anyone as elegant – though I didn't know that word at the time. He wore a black Derby hat, a suit, vest shirt and tie and a fine woolen overcoat. He called us over, bought four sandwiches, told us his name was Louis Norton and that he was looking for a place to open a dry-goods store. He also asked about a place to sleep. The hotel was full, but we thought *Ma* and *Da* might like the rent, so we took him home with us. It was muddy and slippery getting up to the cabin. We carried Mr. Norton's suitcases. He was about the same age as *Da*, but when our father came home from working his claim we saw the great difference between a city man and a dirty, hardworking miner.

"*Ma* and *Da* took a liking to him. They cleaned out the woodshed and caulked the gaps between logs so Mr. Norton would have a warm place to sleep. It was real cozy and he said liked it. He asked us girls to show him around, so we showed him the creek, and the old Indian ruin, and introduced him to some of the prospectors. Arthur Schultz made our parents mad by saying they should watch Mr. Norton around their young girls. He was so obviously a fine gentleman it was ridiculous.

"After supper, each day, we sat and talked. *Ma* and *Da* told him the gold was petering out, and even though we never had a strike, we'd have to move on. It didn't take long for Mr. Norton to know Rockridge wasn't the place for a new store.

"One day he asked Mother and Daddy to come to Chicago and work for him at his store. Daddy said he had one last hunch he wanted to try. Mr. Norton couldn't see any reason we girls didn't come right away. He said his wife would help us get enrolled in school. Sis was eighteen and wouldn't think of going to school. Besides, she was in love with a young miner so she decided to marry him and go wherever he went.

"To me, though, going to the big city to school sounded like an adventure. My parents thought I was a good learner and could do well, and of course I needed polish; Mr. Norton would be just the person to see I got it. I packed my extra dress in a gunny-sack, and Sis and the parents saw us off. After several days, we arrived in Chicago in the middle of the night and because Mr. Norton had sent a telegram from up the line we were met at the station by a long, black automobile. We went directly to his store. Mr. Norton unlocked the door and took me in for what he thought of as proper clothing and outfitted me then and there. I felt all grown up. The clothes were pretty, even though they kind of put me in mind of the ones the saloon girls wore.

CHAPTER 39

ELLIE

Vera kept talking long after Ellie's heart had slid into her throat. Now she wanted the tale to go back to being a secret, but it was too late. Elegant Mr. Louis Norton had used her mother and discarded her. The result was that Ellie was illegitimate. She knew bad names existed for children whose parents weren't married, but she never dreamed that they could apply to her. And to have had her mother hurt like that – to have such a wholly self-centered man for a father — well, she wanted to crawl under the bed and stay, never to be seen again.

"After a few months, Mr. Norton had his chauffer drive me to the convent, and that's how you came to be born there," said Vera. "Now, maybe you understand why I never told you."

When her mother reached for her arm, Ellie steeled herself against moving away. How could anyone be so foolish and naïve, she wondered? Then she recalled that her mother had been only sixteen-years-old when she was duped and manipulated by that evil man. She was pregnant and friendless in the big city.

"The nuns were good to me considering I got myself into all this trouble, but I still felt lonely, and I wanted to keep you. You were the only one born there that week. They planned to send you away to some rich people who wanted a baby. The night sister, however, fell asleep, so I wrapped you in a blanket and escaped through the court-yard. We needed a place to sleep, so right away I looked for a job. I'll always thank God for sending us to the Williams family who ran a pub on skid row. I reminded them of their daughter, who had recently died in childbirth so they gave me a waitressing job and room and board. They insisted I wait a week to begin work, then because you were a newborn, they let you sleep in a big box behind the bar. You were such a good baby. You were happy and you made everyone who saw you smile.

"I wrote my folks and waited for an answer, but instead they came to Chicago to find me. We decided not to meet with Mr. Norton now that we knew what he was. *Da* got a job in the stockyards and *Ma* worked in a general store. By then we had a small apartment and I was able to look after you and the housekeeping during the day. At night your grandmother and grandad took care of you while I continued to work for the Williamses. Eventually by saving and pooling our cash we were able to buy a small, neighborhood store." Vera's voice held tears.

"Dear Mother, I had no idea. A young girl who had never been away from home just wouldn't know. Shouldn't your parents have been more wary?" Ellie now patted the hand resting next to her on the bed.

"I've thought about it over the years, of course," said Vera. "But I never had much confidence in myself. I keep trying to think what I might have done different. But if I'm honest, I got to say, I've always been so glad to have a beautiful and good child like you that I could never regret having you and keeping you."

"Now I understand why you always warned me about men, especially older men. You wanted me to avoid that kind of a situation. Sometimes I felt confused because it seemed as if Grandmother was trying to marry me off to a rich politician, and you seemed reluctant for me to go anywhere with a boy at all. I am sorry you never married, never had a life of your own. Thanks for loving me and looking after me all my life. You were always there quietly in the background.

Vera took hold of Ellie's hand and kissed it. Ellie's heart flooded with love, understanding and compassion. She gently squeezed the hard-working hand of her mother.

"I love you, Mother," she whispered.

CHAPTER 40

ELLIE

"Now tell me about your life in the mountains," said Vera.

Ellie thought a minute, then decided that since she and her mother were starting a new, freer relationship she could tell her something she had not spoken of to anyone.

"I've been teaching the children's Sunday School class at the Community Church in town, even though I don't feel qualified." Vera made an *hmm*, noise which encouraged Ellie to go on.

"We have Bible stories and learn about Jesus and His time on earth. That's the way I think of it — a short time on earth to show us that He was human like us, and at the same time He was God and the Holy Spirit. My theology is scanty, but I've had an experience that I want to tell you about."

"Tell me," said Vera turning toward her daughter.

"Well," Ellie took a deep breath and let it out. "Sunday before last, we came across a scripture that said, 'To the praise of the glory of His grace, wherein he hath made us accepted in the beloved...' Those words – *accepted in the beloved* stuck with me. I decided to ask God what they meant. Suddenly everything I'd been reading and feeling began to make sense. I knew that in spite of my selfishness, God loved and accepted *me*, and it had something to do with Jesus' dying on the cross, though I don't fully understand that part yet."

"I'm not much of a scholar, you know, dear." Vera's brow furrowed as she concentrated on what Ellie was saying.

"I can only tell you what happened to me. The more I thought about Him the more I felt He wanted for a friend. Does that sound strange?" Vera shook her head no. "I asked one of the older boys in the class what I should do and he told me that Jesus died in my place. He helped me through a prayer. When I looked up, the world was shining. The things that had bothered me didn't bother me anymore. I felt tenderness toward folks I hadn't even liked. And the funny thing was, I knew it wasn't my love I was feeling, but God's."

When Ellie stopped talking long enough to look over at her mother, she saw that Vera slept. For an instant she understood how God must have felt all those years when she had ignored him. *But,* she consoled herself. *At least I tried to tell her. Someday I'll tell her again, and she will understand.*

CHAPTER 41

ALDON

It was time for fall round-up, and Aldon was anxious to move the cattle down the mountain before they decided to move themselves. The three-year-old cows had such a strong homing instinct that if no one came for them by the end of summer they'd start down on their own. He knew if that happened the cattle could fall off cliffs, get caught in brush, or be attacked by predators. He had never lost an animal in the process and he wasn't about to start now.

Checking to see that everyone was equipped for the trip, he looked first at Ellie and his heart did cartwheels. She wore her new Stetson and a pair of jeans that would fit a young lad. She had on her dainty leather gloves with his leather sheepskin jacket, well not his anymore. All riders wore multi-purpose bandanas around their necks, even Ellie's Granddad who had come along because of Aldon's earlier invitation. They could use them for carrying freshly caught fish or wild strawberries — not both at the same time, of course. A bandana would keep dust out of their noses or double as a washrag, also it could be handy as a bandage or tourniquet.

Aldon wore his Colt 45s in their holsters slung at hip level and his bullets snugged into the slots of his ammunition belt around his waist. His rifle fit snugly in its case under the stirrup fender.

"You look ready for anything," Aldon said, as he watched Ellie gracefully mount Susie Q. He was proud of her. She had learned so much and so had he. She neither looked at him nor smiled. He'd heard of broken hearts, but he'd never had a taste of one before.

Aldon never got tired of heading out after the cattle when the air was as crisp and pure as cold apple cider, and the leaves on the aspens twinkled silver and gold. As they climbed, he saw more wildflowers than he'd ever seen before. A small patch of snow in perpetual shade had glacier lilies growing near it, while a stump at the top of a rise grew Columbines at its base. He must remember to tell Ellie they were the state flower – that is if she ever stopped ignoring him. They passed Mirror Lake where the mountains reflected in the lake were perfect duplicates of the ones that towered above. The day passed quickly and by the time they got to the line cabin it was almost dark.

Aldon built up the campfire and stood watching while Ellie hooked a pot of beans onto the hanging trivet.

"Will you walk up to the beaver dam with me?" he asked her. "It'll take a while for supper to get warmed up. Kenny can stir the beans and keep them from burning."

Ellie sighed, but still wouldn't look at him.

"Come on, please." He tugged on her jacket sleeve. "I want so badly to talk to you, for a bit."

"Oh all right," she shrugged. "Let's go." She followed silently as he led up the trail.

When they got to the pond she looked around and he could tell she was remembering the last time they were here. They sat down on the warm, flat rock and looked at each other.

"The thing is," he began, "I'm praying hard about developing some self-control."

"You don't have to do it on my account," Ellie said. "I'm not going to be around here that long.

"What?" he jerked his head toward her and stared. He felt as if his blood had stopped circulating. "You're leaving?"

"I don't want you to feel like you did something wrong. You were trying to keep the peace and that was part of your job as a community leader. I'm not exactly pleased with the idea people have of me now, but Enrico has treated me respectfully since then. You didn't think I did anything to encourage him, did you? I didn't mean to." She pressed her lips together.

"No! He didn't need any encouragement. He thought he should have everything his way — we all think like that sometimes, I suppose. But I want to know…am I driving you away?" For the second or third time in his adult life Aldon felt tears coming to his eyes.

"No. I'm going partly because of the weather. I don't want to be here in the wintertime. It's cold enough in Chicago to freeze your toes off, and I hear it's as bad in this place. The ranch won't need me. I'd just get in the way."

"But where are you going? Winter's pretty common most everywhere."

"I'm thinking about California." She ran her fingers through her hair and then smoothed it down.

CHAPTER 42

ALDON

Aldon leaned back supporting himself with a hand on the flat rock. Because Ellie was already peeved with him, he didn't interrupt her to point out the beaver swimming toward its lodge with a stick in its mouth.

"It's warm in California in winter and I figure I could get a job." Ellie wasn't looking at him which showed she knew he was hurting, but he certainly wasn't going to tip his hand in any way. He'd be as polite as a stranger, get to camp and begin preparing to lose her forever.

"Can't blame you for that. My brother, Bill, loves it out there." He forced his words past the lock in his throat.

"Why don't you go too?" Now she looked quickly at him and away again as if she'd said something unseemly.

"Somebody has to stay here and look after the ranch. Aunt Gertrude's got a gentleman friend now. New man in town, lawyer, widower. She's going to get married, and Nancy doesn't want to be in their way, so she's coming back to the ranch. But she and Molly can't run it by themselves. If we didn't have the Solanos, we wouldn't be able to pay off the loans we've been forced to get..." Aldon paused. When he resumed, his voice was low and gravelly. "Maybe you'll run into Bill out there. He's in Hollywoodland. Is that close to where you want to be?"

"I think so," she answered. "I did some reading. Los Angeles has a good climate. There seems to be plenty of jobs."

"What would you work at then, doin' hair?" he asked.

"Probably, something like that." Her blues eyes looked into his and he clenched his teeth to keep his feelings at bay.

"Maybe Bill could help you get a job in the movies. They need people to do hair, don't they?" He forced himself to smile.

"Yes, and they might need more wranglers and stunt men. Is there any chance Bill would want to come home any time soon?" Now, Ellie's eyes held pleading that threw him as if he'd been bucked off a mean bull and was going to get gored. He decided to speak reasonably, rationally, as if her questions didn't affect him in the least. It was like trying not to scare a frightened filly away.

"I don't know. I suppose he might. He could run the ranch, for sure. He's got a girlfriend now. But I can't ask him to do it. He's been sending money right along." Aldon heard the faint sounds of the cow bell and knew it was time for supper.

"I guess we might as well head back." Ellie said.

"Yep," Aldon wiped the back of his hand under his cheek bone and started back down the trail. Ellie followed, meek and quiet.

CHAPTER 43

ALDON

The trip down the mountain was easy until they got into a sloping meadow where the herd fanned out. There, without warning two horsemen came over a rise yelling and shooting their side-arms. The Herefords took off in a stampede, leaving no time to go after the hecklers.

Riding fast on both sides of the herd, the men set themselves to stopping the stampede. First they had to get them into a mill. It wouldn't do for them to fall into a draw and break their necks or get lost and have to be rounded up all over again. Kenny and Aldon rode next to the head of the stampede slowly forcing them to change their course and double back. After a few heart-stopping moments, the beasts melted into a swirling, red and white tornado, and were forced to slow to a standstill. Eventually they settled down and began to graze. Aldon took the first deep breath he'd had since the stampede began.

"You can start on down again, Mr. Morgan," Aldon rode to the wagon with Susie Q in tow. Do you mind riding Ellie's horse?" he asked. He dipped his hat in thanks to the older man who got down off the wagon and mounted Susie Q.

Aldon tied Chief to the back of the chuck wagon, and took his place on the seat next to Ellie.

"I'm glad everyone is safe." She touched his face with her warm, slender hand and all at once Aldon felt as full of ginger as a day old colt.

"Who were those men?" Ellie asked.

"Probably the squatters that were at the ranch with Enrico the other night," Aldon gave the reins a shake to remind the mules they weren't allowed to graze along the way.

Why would they do something like that? We could have been hurt or killed." Ellie leaned against him as though seeking reassurance.

"Nah," he shook his head and then looked directly at her. "It's all in a day's work."

"But, what if one of us had died?" Her eyes pooled with unshed tears.

"That would have been a shame, don't you think?" He put his arm around her shoulders and gave her a gentle squeeze.

"Why would it have been a shame?" He guessed maybe she was looking for reassurance. "We've got a lot of living to do." He clicked his tongue at the mules to move along now that they were on more even ground.

"But what's the use of living if you're not happy?" She asked.

"You're not happy?" He hadn't known that. He'd thought she was just mad at him.

"Not really," she answered rubbing her hand on her jeans.

"Don't you know? It's, it's..." there was a sob in her voice... because we're at odds with each other."

"You may be at odds with me, but I'm not at odds with you," he said.

"You're not?" She found a handkerchief in the jacket pocket and dabbed at her eyes.

"Haven't you noticed who has been doing the ignoring?" He pulled the brim of his hat down a quarter of an inch.

"You walked off when I was trying to talk to you after church."

"All right, I'm here now. What did you want to say?" Aldon pushed the hat back a bit and gave her his full attention.

"Having men fight over me was embarrassing." She put her hands over her face.

"Didn't I tell you I was sorry?" He thought he had explained how he felt, but obviously he hadn't said the words she needed to hear. Would dealing with this woman ever become easy and commonplace? He doubted it but he knew he'd keep on trying.

"Out here we call a man responsible for his own actions even if he's sick or drunk." Aldon, shifted and wrapped his hand around hers. He held it against his chest which seemed to have some kind of a flutter in it.

"Besides, you could have hurt him." Ellie's hand cuddled into his.

"There's no harm in a bully getting hurt if he's misbehaving, especially toward a lady like yourself." He knew he sounded gruff.

"Is that what you think he is… a bully?" She tugged, but he held on to her hand.

"Maybe, but I have to be honest with you, I wasn't sorry about interfering with that young man." She tried again to pull away, but he went on talking. "I was, though, very sorry it upset you. I know fighting isn't right or good, but sometimes men must look after women and…

"Are you saying I don't know how to look after myself?" Ellie's voice rose slightly.

"Anyhow, I never hit him. He passed out while I was dragging him away." He tried to tell her the truth, hoping she'd listen.

"You didn't hit him? But he was unconscious when you threw him in the pick-up."

"No ma'am, I wouldn't hit a shrimp like him. You ever heard of, *pick on somebody your own size*?" Aldon shook his head amazed at her lack of understanding. "Besides, why do you care what other people think?"

"You don't care what people think of you?" She asked.

"I care what you think." He gently rested their joined hands on the seat.

"Why?" She sighed.

"First 'cause you're a good woman."

"What else?"

"You're easy on the eyes." He flashed her a smile.

"You like the way I look?" Ellie, who was sitting hip to hip with him scooted a bit closer. Knowing he'd fall off if he moved, he sat as still as if he were watching a herd of wild mustangs grazing.

"Sure I do." Maybe they were getting somewhere now. He held his breath.

"And?" Her voice went up on a singsong note.

"I got fond of you." He gently squeezed her hand.

"Why did you stop talking to me, then? People can't read each other's minds. We've got to communicate."

"Everything I said seemed to make things worse."

She thought and nodded. He wondered if she might be getting angry all over again.

Aldon turned loose of her hand, removed his hat, scratched his head, leaving tufts of champagne colored hair sticking up like bull horns on the front of his head, and put the hat back on over them. Silence fell and after a long haul to the ranch, the mules pulled the wagon into the barn.

CHAPTER 44

ALDON

Now that they were home from round-up, it was time for Signora Solano's musicale. While the ladies primped, Aldon asked Ellie's grandfather to help take the dining room and kitchen chairs into the big front parlor. Seraphina, who had been roaming the house looking for something to do, asked if she, and the kitten she clutched to her chest, could help. Aldon glanced at the older man who grinned and winked. Aldon could read Mr. Morgan's heart then, and knew he was remembering his granddaughter's childhood.

"Sure you can. Dust with this." Mr. Morgan took a large white handkerchief from his pocket and gave it to Seraphina, who put the kitten down and began to run the cloth over the baseboards. The kitten, doing his part, crouched, wiggled, and pounced making Seraphina's giggles tinkle through the room like a merry brook.

Loud voices alerted Aldon that his cousins had arrived with Eva and Olga from town. When he heard the chiming voices of the young women against the roar of the men, he thought back to two small pigtailed girls arriving for the beginning of school not knowing how to speak English. As he strode to the back door to greet them, he recalled that the girls had worn home-made traditional German costumes for school plays. *They're wearing them still* he thought as he approached. *But bigger sizes and more filled out.* From the way the girls clung to Dieter's and Joe's arms, Aldon sensed that their bachelor days were limited. Instead of teasing with a knowing look, he stifled his envy.

Dieter, who was as tall as Aldon and much beefier, jammed his shoulder against his cousin's, delighting in putting him off balance so he'd have to take a step. Dieter had been doing that since they were ten years old and Aldon had never thought it funny.

"Did you call Sheriff Oates?" Dieter asked.

"Come out here, for a minute," said Aldon knowing there would be no talking to the boys as long as they were showing off in front of the girls. Joe followed telling his date to go on in and take his tuba with her. She hefted it willingly, as a stout housewife would hoist a basket of laundry.

The men followed Aldon to the barn where he turned suddenly and said, "I wish you'd keep your mouth shut, for once."

"What are you goin' on about? We got to bring the Sheriff in or get up a posse to go after them squatters. Somebody coulda got hurt, plus don't you know they're the ones what stole those five cattle we're missing." Dieter always spoke his mind. Aldon only hoped none of the other men would hear him. If they did, and formed a posse, somebody would have to talk them out of taking the law into their own hands.

"Yeah," said Joe. "We got to do somethin' "

"Okay, here's what I've been thinking," said Aldon. "Number one, we can't do anything about finding those fellows in the dark. Number two, they aren't going anywhere; they're not what you'd call adventuresome types. They've been on that mountain their whole lives, I doubt if they'd know how to read a map or buy a train ticket."

"We goin' let them go?" Joe asked.

"No, I've already told you, we'll let the sheriff deal with it. We are not going outside the law and we're not going to tell anyone. You got that? So don't' say another word about it." He felt better after making sure they wouldn't stir up trouble he wasn't ready to handle. To change the subject he asked where they had found the tuba and the accordion they had brought."

"Ma took it in her head to clean the attic and when she found the instruments, she told us to get rid of them, but instead we fixed them up. We had to order some new bellows 'cause the mice got at them, but we didn't have no trouble taking them apart and putting them back together."

As they went through the kitchen and into the front parlor, Aldon wondered where Ellie was. He hoped she was all right and that she would be down soon. He tried never to worry, but it was hard to set aside the thought of her leaving the ranch. Knowing nothing in life could compare with the simple happiness of being in her company, he was overwhelmed with grief and helplessness.

Finishing his conversation with his cousins he led the way back to the parlor where practicing and tuning of instruments created chaos. As Mrs. Fitzgerald and her son, Kenny, settled themselves at the piano the room grew still. Coleen and Kenny both played by ear, and they had practiced together most of the boy's life. Their duets were now the sensation of Clifton. When they began the lively, "By the Sea," everyone began to tap their toes.

CHAPTER 45

ALDON

Everyone settled in as Enrico and Lia began to sing an aria, which Aldon thought sounded like cats fighting. He and Ellie followed with, "Whispering Hope on violin and mandolin." They had discussed playing one of their impromptu jazz pieces, but knew it was hard for the older folks to accept unfamiliar music. As they played, Mr. Solano bowed his head and held his hands in the prayer position. Aldon, glancing up from his instrument thought, *Pray for Ellie and me.*

Nancy had a piano piece, to which Seraphina danced in a new yellow dress Lia had bought her. The four person oompha group drew raves of applause and laughter as they played a lively polka, thus bringing the musical to a joyous close.

Some of the people filed into the kitchen, but Aldon and Ellie were inundated with compliments and handshakes. Eventually, people stepped between them leaving Aldon standing by himself in the parlor. *Might as well straighten up,* he thought. He took the extra chairs the dining room and kitchen all the while searching for Ellie. He never found her. Finally he went found Molly to ask where Ellie was. Before he could say a word, Molly grabbed his arm.

"Come with me, I want to show you something," she said. She took the lead stopping at the closed door to the back porch. Staring out the window and jerking her thumb to signal him to look she stepped back to give him the full view.

Aldon stared at a scene he had expected never to witness. There, with her back pressed against the coats stood Ellie with Enrico leaning against her and holding her wrists above her head. Ellie stood as still as a rabbit with her eyes closed tight. At the sight Aldon turned and made his way out the front door without hesitating or looking back.

In a blind rage, he saddled Chief, urging him to run, which his obedient horse was happy to do. They scrambled up the mountainside until it got so steep that Chief had to slow down. Aldon wanted to ride forever, trying to cool the angry fever inside, but he calmed himself enough to realize that he didn't want to ride his horse to death. When they arrived at the cabin, he tied Chief to the hitching post and strode through the front door, slamming it behind him.

The night was so dark he wondered why he hadn't fallen off the shelf road or got stuck in a gully on his way here. He knew he had no chance of sleeping, so he found matches in a tobacco tin, struck one, turned up the wick on the kerosene lamp and lit it. As he laid the King Albert container on the table, he wondered how long it would be before the pack-rats returned and stole it. Was there no safety anywhere? He sat at the table with his head in his hands. Then looking up he saw the Bible tucked under a shelf, and pulled it out. He opened it at random and read Psalm 51.

"Have mercy upon me, O God, according to thy lovingkindness: according unto the multitude of thy tender mercies, blot out my transgressions. Wash me thoroughly from mine iniquity, and cleanse me from my sin,"

He paused, calmer now, knowing His heavenly Father had promised never to ignore, his needs, or his deeds. Suddenly he recalled Pastor Rudd's suggestion that people who had something on their minds could write letters to God, who is always waiting to hear from them. *That's it,* Aldon thought *who better to talk to than my heavenly Father?*

He opened the drawer and found a piece of scratch paper and a stub of pencil. One side of the paper had a list on it. He recognized the writing immediately. It was Ellie's. She had written the names and descriptions of the wildflowers he had told her about at round-up: She had underlined "Monument Plant: grows only in moist years, waits between twenty and sixty years for a full rainy season to bloom again.

She had listed the three colors of Indian Paintbrush: lemon, rose, and red. She had written down everything he had told her! He felt a tightness in his shoulders as the anger boiled again. Why did she write it all down as if she cared about him when all along she planned to choose Enrico?

CHAPTER 46

ALDON

When Aldon realized he was shivering, he thought he'd better get the quilt over his legs. He found a board and started writing his letter to God.

Dear Heavenly Father,

The line-cabin is chilly, but I don't mean to complain. I came away so fast after seeing Ellie and Enrico that I forgot my jacket, my bedroll, and my sidearm. When Molly took me to see what was going on between the two of them, she had my best interests at heart, but, Lord, I wish I'd never seen it. Sir, now that I have a chance to start thinking instead of reacting, I know I'm as desperate as a misused bronc and as unseeing as a newborn kitten. I need your help.

As you know, heavenly father, we got a letter from Bill that told us he was heading home. I'm sure you know that he has a wife and that he has been married for almost a year. I wish I had known he'd be here to take care of the ranch. I could have asked Ellie to marry me. I could have gone to California and got a job as wrangler with the movies. It's all too late. Ellie will be gone. Joe and Dieter will marry, and I'll be alone for the rest of my life. I should have told Ellie that I love her. I don't care if she is a mechanician from back East, a flapper, or a society lady. She is smart, kind, loving, and wonderful, and I was a fool to miss my chance with her. Protect her from becoming heart-broken please, Lord.

Now, as always when he finished telling the Lord how he felt, and asking him for help, he began to feel his spirits lift. A different concern seeped into his mind. He recalled a pastor once saying, "Do the next thing." What was the next thing? Oh, yes, he had to deal with the rustlers. He sat with the pencil in his hand until he could think out a plan. Suddenly the whole story was clear. He jumped up and checked the cabin, then seeing again his letter, picked it up. He turned it over, and read Ellie's list again. Knowing no one could see him, he lifted it and gently kissed the place where she had written, *Monument Plant*. Then as he scanned his own writing, more peace flooded into his soul. Folding the paper into a small packet, he snapped it into the breast pocket of his shirt where it would be safe. He could read it again or write more if he started to slide into the quicksand of self-pity. He whispered another prayer to the only person in the cabin with him, the Holy Spirit.

He grabbed his hat, and ran out to Chief. He was embarrassed to see that he had left him saddled. He'd never forgotten before. "Sorry boy, I get you some extra oats when we get to town."

As he rode he tried to put thoughts of Ellie out of his mind. One thing he did know, though: he would always love it. Then he prayed some more. *But, I also know, Lord that it won't do any good to try to hang on, even in my mind. She has made her choice and I have to live with it.*

His God assignment, as he saw it, became more urgent as he headed down the mountain. He must get to Sheriff Oates before someone from the round-up, probably Dieter, got on the party line started talking. Aldon knew the men who lived here, knew they'd never give a supposed rustler a second chance. They would, without thought or conscience, become outlaws in order to protect their livelihood.

He and Chief picked their way down the upper slopes and onto the road past the ranch. Maybe Ellie was already in the kitchen, but he wasn't ready to see her, so instead of stopping for an automobile, he urged Chief who was acting frisky to move past at a canter.

He rode through the sleeping town to the church where Quentin

Rudd had recently risen from his bed. The pastor invited Aldon to stay for breakfast, but all he'd come for was to tell him where he'd be in case anyone came looking.

When he stopped at the Fitzgeralds, he asked Mr. Fitzgerald to take Chief to the livery, unsaddle him and comb him down. He walked the few blocks to the railroad station and boarded the morning train. He slept a while until they got going then he stepped onto the caboose balcony to remember the last time he was on the train. It was a short trip, and soon he was on the main street of Artesia, leaning against the hitching post across the street from the Sheriff's office, waiting for Oates to come down and unlock the door.

CHAPTER 47

ELLIE

Waking late the morning after the musicale, Ellie went to the kitchen to help with breakfast. "Where's Aldon?" she asked. Molly didn't seem to have heard as she scrubbed away at the top of the stove. Ellie repeated her question.

"I haven't seen him this morning. Chief is gone, so I suppose he's went, too." Molly words were harsh and crisp like chopped ice on frigid morning.

"Maybe he went for Sherriff Oates." Ellie asked.

"Why would he do that?" Molly didn't look up from her work, and Ellie wondered if the older woman was annoyed with her.

"Oh, he didn't explain?"

"There was no time for him to tell me anything. He took off right after the refreshments, last night. "Opening the oven door and getting down on one knee, Molly applied her energy to the interior.

"What's wrong? Didn't you sleep well?" Ellie asked.

"You'll have to ask Aldon." Molly got up and washed the rag in a bowl of ammonia. "It ain't none of my business."

"Molly, please. I can't ask him if he's not here."

"We saw you last night." Molly, rested her fists on her hips with the rag hanging down.

"What did you see?" Ellie took a deep breath to slow her racing heart, but she feared she knew what Molly and Aldon had seen, and probably misinterpreted.

"Me and Aldon saw you and that Eye-talian spooning."

"Spooning? Ellie!" Grandmother entered the kitchen. "How could you. Your mother and I taught you better than that!"

"You're a real packet, Missy." Molly, ignored Hester, and glared straight into Ellie's eyes. "You and Enrico smooching on the porch. For your information, young lady, we don't like such goings on in this house." Molly pursed her lips.

"Enrico mistakenly thought I'd appreciate his attentions," Ellie said.

"A likely story!" said Molly. "I've seen you two laughing and flirting."

"All right, then. What did you think you saw?" Ellie motioned for her grandmother to come to her side.

"I don't think…I know!" Molly folded her arms over her chest still holding the rag, and ready for battle. "You were all cozy against the coats and…and… I can't say more."

"You didn't see what happened next, did you?" Ellie's lips felt dry. *Please, Lord, help me.*

"Aldon saw it too, that's probably why he took off without telling anyone where he was going." Molly tossed her head back and sniffed.

"You should have watched a little longer." Ellie said.

"So, now you think I'm nothing but a busybody, do you?"

"No, I think you're a good woman trying to protect your family." Ellie didn't want to shock the two older women, but she knew she had to defend herself.

"He was forcing me against the coats. If you had watched for a few more seconds you would have seen me knee him," said Ellie.

"You mean you kicked him where he lives?" Molly's mouth opened and closed, her eyes grew large. She paused and a small, "ha," escaped her lips. She then began to laugh in short bursts as if she were trying to hold it in. "You didn't want anything to do with him?"

"That's what they taught us in the ambulance corps where we worked with all kinds of men." Ellie smiled at Molly's amusement.

"So the young whippersnapper finally got his comeuppance. Did you hurt him good?" Molly said relishing each word.

Ellie barely nodded.

"I see," said Molly satisfied. Ellie knew Aldon's aunt did not believe in apologizing, but that was all right as long as they could remain friends.

"You ought to be ashamed of yourself for thinking my Ellie would spoon with anyone." Now Grandmother Hester hugged Ellie to her side.

"Yes, ma'am." Molly reached over and patted Ellie's shoulder. "I understand now."

"You did nothing wrong, dear," Grandmother said.

"I'm going up to the pond, and see if I can find Aldon. He must think I've deserted him. Grandmother, will you ask Mother to help Molly cook breakfast?" Hester nodded and at the same time, Lia came into the kitchen.

"I'm going with you," said Lia.

"No! Why?"

"Because I have to tell him something," she said.

"I want to go alone." Ellie spoke in a voice that she hoped would hold Lia off.

"I'm tired," Grandmother said. "I'll send your mother down." She left the room walking slowly and Ellie saw that Grandmother was going to need extra care for the next several years. When had she grown so old? Her hair was white, her face lined, and her shoulders stooped.

I'll have to think about that later, Ellie thought. *Right now I'm going to find Aldon.*

CHAPTER 48

ELLIE

Leaving the horses at the bottom of the trail, Ellie and Lia hurried toward the waterfall. When they turned the corner, they were surprised to see two figures standing at the edge of the pond with their backs to them. One was the tall one in the stovepipe hat and the other a short and round fellow with a bushy beard. Ellie had seen them both in the barnyard, with Enrico, the night the masked men came. Ellie's foot dislodged a rock on the trail, and the men swung around.

"Well, looky there," said the short one. His voice was high-pitched and gleeful, with a touch of innocence in it. "Here they is. Can you believe our luck? Grab them before they get away."

By the time Ellie and Lia realized the men meant to seize them, it was too late to escape. Both tried to fight them off, but they ended up held fast by their wrists. One for each man.

"Gimme me that one, too," the tall man grabbed Lia away from the other man and held a wrist in each hand.

"Let go of me." Lia struggled but couldn't pull loose.

"Ha ha." The tall man said. "Quite the feisty one, ain't you? That should make Ma happy. She can beat up on somebody besides us."

Remembering Granddad's folksy saying, *you can catch more flies with honey than with vinegar,* Ellie counseled herself to relax and tap into the power of God that she had been experiencing lately. "May I inquire, sir, what you are going to do with us?" she said in a cool voice.

"This here bean-pole is my brother Furstus, and I'm Lastus." The hairy man, who resembled a bear, smoothed his beard, grinned a wide grin, and made a bow. "He was first- born and I was last-born. That's why Ma called us Furstus and Lastus. Do you get it? What we're doing here is setting us up some brides. Mama needs help scraping deerskins, washing clothes, and cleaning the fireplace. She don't want no help with cooking, but she *is* looking for some grandchilren and she expects me and Furstus to supply 'em." He bowed.

"Stop jawing and get down there where we left them horses," Furstus said. He pulled them along until Lia stumbled. Ellie steadied her and made a shushing sound to quiet her. She figured the less noise they made, the less annoyance they would cause.

Susie Q reared once when she saw and smelled the interlopers. Ellie expected her to bolt, but when her hooves came down she stood quivering. "Hold on, girl, it's okay," Ellie said softly. Susie Q stood still long enough for Ellie to mount. Furstus tied Ellie's wrists to the saddle-horn. Lastus threw Lia face down over Ribbon's saddle. Ellie was startled into objecting. "Don't do that to her. You'll hurt her." The heavy-set man frowned, but the other one laughed.

As they rode uphill, Ellie recognized the terrain from former trips into the mountains. The caves she had seen from the shelf road could be approached in a round-about way and soon the women found themselves off the horses and sitting on the cold stone floor of a cavern.

"Take these ropes off immediately!" Lia demanded, her voice growing stronger as she began to speak rapid Italian as she released her ire.

"Let's kill them and get it over with," Furstus pulled out his Bowie knife and licked his lips. He then gave a high-pitched laugh that seemed calibrated to terrify everyone within a five mile radius.

CHAPTER 49

ALDON

After what seemed like a long day, Aldon and Sheriff Oates arrived at the tumble-down cabin of Mrs. Stump Slater.

'Hello the cabin," Aldon shouted as the two men dismounted. Immediately the door opened. A small, bent woman hobbled from the house, lifted an ancient shotgun and aimed at the Sheriff's left foot. Aldon placed a restraining hand on the Sheriff's shoulder knowing Oate's hair-trigger temper from riding the range with him in bygone days.

"What you want?" the old lady asked in a quavering voice.

"We're looking for your sons, ma'am," said Aldon.

"How do you know my sons?" Mrs. Slater asked.

"The law wants them for questioning." said Oates.

"Them no-good stupid-heads ain't here," she said.

"Can you tell us where they are?" The sheriff asked. He gripped the handle of his sidearm.

"The last I saw 'em they was riding downhill talking about bringing home some brides," said Mrs. Slater.

"Who would those brides be, do you suppose?" Aldon sensed a letting down in the old woman as if she had carried the boys about as far as she could.

Where did they go?" Oates asked.

"Lastus took a fancy to a dark-headed hussy, that's all I know." The woman's mouth hung slack and she shook her head. "They don't tell me nothin'. All they do is eat, hunt, and fight."

"I know where they're hiding!" Aldon said with sudden inspiration. He mounted again and Oates, followed his lead. "It's not far."

"Do you know what hussy she was talking about?" The sheriff's horse set down its hooves carefully as they existed through the weedy pasture that covered the front yard.

"I do, and if they took that one, they'll be real anxious to give her back."

"Used to having her own way, is she?" Oates stopping talking then as Aldon urged Chief through the aspens.

After half an hour they came to the shelf road. "Hold up here." Aldon said stopping. "We've got to plan our maneuvers."

"We ain't had nothing to eat all day," Oates complained.

"You want to open the beans we got before we left town." Aldon reached his left hand back and patted the saddle bag.

"I ain't eating no more canned beans if I have to starve." Oates's stomach rumbled as if it didn't agree with his statement.

"Keep quiet. Let's figure this thing out." said Aldon.

"You're not sweet on your boss's wife are you?" Oates asked with raised eyebrows.

"Good Grief! Whatever ever gave you that lame-brained idea?"

"You're in such an all-fired hurry, I thought you had a personal stake in the outcome of this here enterprise."

"Maybe I do, but it's not the boss's wife. I can tell you that for certain sure. Signora Solano hardly ever goes anywhere without her sidekick, Ellie, and if Ellie's there we have a better chance of collecting those women because Ellie's got horse-sense."

"That's a relief. It wouldn't do for you to be sweet on a girl with nothing horsy about her at all." He grinned, but kept his distance. "I always knew once you fell in love that would be it." Ignoring him, Aldon gave a loud, two note, *bob-white* whistle that sounded like the real thing.

In a moment an answering call came winging over the hill.

"There now," said Aldon, "I taught her that, isn't she something?"

"Yeah, except this ain't mating season."

"We'll sneak up and get them away from those Slater boys." Aldon was the one grinning now.

CHAPTER 50

ELLIE

After Lastus and Furstus put Lia and Ellie into a large cave at the edge of a cliff they unpacked the horses, talking as if the women couldn't hear them.

"That black-headed one is my little darling. You touch her and you're dead. I saw her first a long time ago when she was making a pitcher at the pond and she hurt herself and fainted. He walked to the women and leaned down to kiss Lia's cheek. She tried to hit out, but he dodged the swing. You know durn well I want a woman of my own, and I'm picking this one." He went on talking.

"Oh, shut up you low-down ugly old skunk." Furstus shook his head. "Now you women, if either of you can cook, don't tell Ma. She'd take it hard if she thought we didn't like her cooking and had brought in someone else to do it."

"Neither of us can really cook," said Ellie quickly. Lia's expression said she was about to object, but Ellie frowned and Lia subsided.

Lastus pulled a brown square from his pocket and bit off a chunk filling his cheek. He held what looked like a hard cake up to Lia. "Have a chaw, sweetie?" he inquired. Lia shuddered and shook her head.

"I'm goin to get some more fire wood," said Furstus walking down the side of the mountain.

"Don't you like this kind of tabaccy? It's Ma's favorite" said Lastus refusing to be interrupted in the middle of his courting game.

"Lia might like you better, young man, if you weren't so hairy." She nudged the other woman to let her know she had a plan.

"Might you, Miss?" He looked at Lia sitting on the cave's floor.

"I might," she said, cutting her eyes at Ellie and then quickly back at Lastus.

"Good, I'll give you a haircut and a shave." Ellie said.

"You don't look like you got nothing to shave a body with.'" said Lastus.

Ellie recalled Aldon wanting to hang a gun belt on her and wished she had accepted it. She had no idea whether she could actually shoot a man, but she thought if they made a move to hurt her or Lia, she'd be willing to try.

"I can cut your hair with that knife." She indicated the knife in a scabbard attached to his belt. "If it's sharp enough, I can shave you too." Just in time, Ellie recalled Granddad's mention of the pride men took in the sharpness of their blades.

"Ya got a deal," said Lastus. He pulled the knife out of its holder, and began to rub the blade on a small whetstone from his shirt pocket. "I always keeps my knives as sharp as my brain in case one a them bears gets mad when we're trying to kill it."

Lia fanned her face with her hand and Ellie knew it was a way of saying, what a lot of bologna.

"All right, hand it over." Ellie ordered." He slapped the knife handle into her palm. "Sit on that rock. We'll get you shaved."

When he was clean-shaven she picked up a strand of greasy hair, sliced it off and started a pile at her feet. She kept cutting until the blade got dull, then she allowed him to sharpen it again. Once a tangle of curls had been tamed into a short, military cut, she angled the broad blade into the last rays of the sun so he could see a reflection. He turned his head this way and that and ran his hand over his cheek. Having been shorn, he looked almost harmless—and much younger.

"Is that me?" he said, his voice full of awe. "Why I'm a right pretty sight, ain't I?"

"How many years have you?" Lia asked, her voice subdued.

"I don't rightly know. 'Round about sixteen. How old are you, Miss Lady?"

"*Trenta,* old enough to be your mama," Lia snapped.

"Oh, no, Ma's a real old lady. You're beautiful and I want you to come home with us. I'll treat you good. I won't let Ma hit you and I won't let Furstus be mean to you. I'll wash all the clothes and I've got a pair of real good sad-irons. I know how to use them, too. I'll save you from all the work I can."

"Oh, Lastus, I can't come with you. I am married all ready and my husband and I are going to have a baby."

"I had no idea, that's wonderful!" Ellie gasped. "Oh, I hope you're all right."

"Yes, I am *sana,* how you say, full of good health. And the bambino, he is so tiny he would not be hurt by such a day." Lia looked smug and rather proud of herself.

CHAPTER 51

ALDON

No one in the cave seemed aware that Aldon and Oates were standing in the opening until Oates, holding a rifle on them, ordered, "Put your hands up!" Then in one fluid move, the three of them, Lia, Ellie, and Lastus sprang to their feet with their hands in the air.

"Oh, we're so glad to see you." Ellie looked straight into Aldon's eyes as if no one else was there. His heart leapt. He stepped up to her, pulled her hands down, wrapped them around his own waist and held her long enough to breathe deeply with relief. She was safe. He'd get her out of here as soon as possible and then he'd leave her alone.

"Ha, ha, you must be glad to see us," Oates said. You girls pack up anything you want to take and we'll be on our way. Where do you suppose that other lout might be by now? Where's your brother, Knothead?" Even though Sheriff Oates had taken command, Lastus would not look at him or acknowledge his presence. The sheriff put handcuffs on the fellow while went to get the horses. When he returned with them everyone mounted except Lastus who was on foot. As they started down, Aldon took out his harmonica and began to play, "Whispering Hope." They rounded a curve and without warning came face to face with the older Slater brother and his horse, coming up the other way. In a split second, Aldon recognized the horse as one of his. That made the other man a horse thief, as well as a kidnapper. Before Aldon could speak or move, the man flung himself off the horse, and rolled down the mountain side. They all heard the sounds of his fall through heavy brush and over large boulders.

When Aldon heard the man splash into the creek and curse, he knew he'd live until someone could come back for him. The horse, which Aldon had named Galaxy, stood immobilized his ears laid back and his eyes wild with fear.

"That's my boy, Galaxy!" Aldon spoke to the horse in a gentle tone and his ears came forward in recognition. "Hold on, you'll be all right now. We'll get you down off this road."

"Ellie, can you help me, please. We need to move Galaxy down the trail backwards."

Ellie slid off Susie Q and crept past the wagon supported by Aldon's hand

"Tell that woman she ain't at a tea-party," yelled Sheriff Oates. Aldon ignored him and dismounted, glad to stretch his muscles.

"Be careful," Lia called. Aldon winced at the intrusion of her voice, but went on to make his way to the horse's tail.

"Gently push on his chest," Aldon told her. "I'll guide him from back here. Slow and gentle," he said. *Good thing I trained him to back up*, Aldon thought.

"You're doing fine. It's not far now. He trusts you, and he's going to keep moving." He felt grateful to Ellie and to God. Finally they reached a place wide enough to turn a horse. "Good work." He breathed deeply, glad to have accomplished the task, happy to be on speaking terms with Ellie again."

CHAPTER 52

ALDON

That evening, at home, Lia insisted everyone eat together at the long table in the kitchen, except Lastus. Aldon took the lad to a storage room on the second floor and handcuffed him to the iron frame of a bed. After the meal, the sheriff and Aldon took a tray up and checked on the prisoner. They then went to the barn to finalize their plans. Oates wanted to go back to the mountain to catch Furtus. Aldon was ready to go too, but his friend insisted he stay and make sure Lastus didn't pull any funny stuff.

"Can you drive Lastus to the jail in Artesia tomorrow? The sheriff's office will pay for gas. He won't give you no trouble. Without his brother, he's just an overgrown kid. I expect he'll get a tongue-lashing from his Ma, though. She won't care what he done, but she'll get mad that he got caught." Oates, now well-fed was able to see the humor in the situation. He left with a happy wave.

Under strict orders not to uncuff Lastus for anything except the outhouse, Aldon fed him supper. Neither of them had a word to say. As Aldon was placing the empty tray outside the door, Lia appeared at the top of the stairs. When Aldon saw her, he looked around for an escape route, but it was too late, he was trapped.

"This Lastus," Lia pulled a small sheaf of folded papers from the pocket of her dress. "I think he was the one that carried me home the first Sunday Ellie was here. I wait until everybody goes to church then I go to the pond to paint. I hear a noise and jump up. My ankle turns, it hurts like fire and out I go. Next thing I recall, I am laid out in the dirt by the kitchen step. When I hobble up to my room and unpack my painting bag these are in it. "She unfolded two sheets of paper with large writing on them.

"Let me hear it," Aldon motioned impatiently for her to read and get it over so he could leave.

"Dear Miss Lady, Ma says me and Furstus needs to find some women. Ma says she is getting old and we need somebody to render bear fat, scrape skins, and tend the fire.

Now, Ma don't care if the women we bring home are ugly or pretty, she wants them to help with the work and give her some gran-chilren to spoil. But to my way of thinking I'd just as soon have some-body with looks and that is you.

You never seen me before, but I live above Spruce Crick Ranch in the mountains. Today I seen you painting by the waterfall and dipping your pretty little fingers in the water. You are one fine figger of a woman. You would do fine for me; Furstus has got to find his own woman. I'm staking my claim on you.

You might wonder how it is I am able to write so good. Well the answer is Ma taught me to read and write. She was smart, but pa wasn't. Ma says I take after him and I'm proud to know it. We never did go to school much except for that one day when Ma left us standing outside the schoolhouse door and the teacher come out and fetched us in. We was already full-growed. At recess the other kids called us Stinky and Fatty so we give them Indian burns. The principal beat us and chucked us out of the school house. Since Ma didn't let us come in on horses we had to walk all the way up the mountain to home, which is a piece.

We never got such a beating from Ma because she's an itty-bitty thing, but she has other ways of torturing us, like no food, so I'd rather take a thrashing from a real man. I don't know why we didn't gang up and fight back. Furstus has been after me about that, but I just didn't feel like hurting the man when it was his school and we didn't belong there. Them folks was too good for the likes of us. You are too, Miss Lady, but I got such a hankering to hold you in my arms, that I'm overlooking that to get you in my camp as fast as I can.

CHAPTER 53

ALDON

"Where is Enrico?" Aldon set the tray on the counter.

"Probably at the saloon, there's no place else for the boy to go." Molly answered.

Aldon began to think about Enrico's whereabouts and how he might be connected with the kidnapping. If the Slater brothers met up with Enrico at the saloon all Signor's he might have told them when round-up was scheduled. He could also have given them ideas of where to look for the women. Aldon remembered what Jesus had said, "If you're not for me, then you're against me" and reckoned the same could be said of Enrico. If he wasn't for the people who lived at the ranch, he must be against them. It would probably be better if he went back to Switzerland or wherever he wanted to be. The kindly Mr. Solano would mourn for a while, but Aldon knew the older man had gained a new vitality and love of life. It looked as if he would fully recover, after all. Maybe Enrico would leave without his grandfather ever knowing how meddlesome he'd been.

"I'm going to check on the kid." Aldon excused himself and climbed the stairs. There, Lastus lay sound asleep spread-eagled, with his wrist cuffed to the iron bedstead. He might have a chance at a decent existence if he could get away from his brother and mother for a while. Maybe the law could send him somewhere and train him for a real job. No use to send him to prison where he could learn how to be a criminal. Maybe he'd talk it over with Ellie. Aldon lay down on the floor next to the bed and went to sleep for what seemed like minutes, but the next thing he knew, the rooster crowed.

When Aldon and Lastus came into the kitchen Ellie was making pancakes. "I figured you'd want an early start," she said putting them one by one on a plate with the pancake flipper. Ellie sounded subdued. "Would I be in the way if I rode along? I've got a hankering to get out of here for a while."

"A hankering? You're talking like a Westerner." His eyes filled with the sight of her golden hair and peachy skin.

"Yes, I think of myself as a Westerner. I've enjoyed my time here." Her eyes filled with tears, but she turned her back and brushed them away. Aldon saw that Lastus was watching Ellie closely. He had probably never seen anything like her. The lad kept his mouth shut, though, which was the first smart thing Aldon had seen him do.

"Do you still plan to leave here?" He asked Ellie, pushing down the dart of fear that lodged in his throat.

"Granddad wants to move on to California." She turned toward him as she spoke. "It's warmer there for Grandmother's arthritis and you know how he has always talked about going West." She set the stack of pancakes on the table.

Aldon said. "My brother tells me California is great, but it does turn cold sometimes, and it gets foggy too." He didn't know why he was arguing with her. She'd made up her mind, but he felt sick even thinking about her leaving.

"How did your prisoner do during the night?" She changed the subject, a clever ploy to avoid another argument. Aldon played along by motioning toward Lastus. "He's okay."

When Aldon put Lastus in the backseat of the flivver he handcuffed him to the steel post that supported the roof. He saw Ellie into the front seat. Over the summer the road had developed so many potholes that everything rattled as they motored along. Ellie looked back then mimed to Aldon that the boy slept.

The minute the car stopped in front of the sheriff's office, Ellie jumped out, and stood waiting for Aldon to unlock Lastus's hand-cuff. All at once the squatter bolted away from Aldon and around the automobile and grabbed Ellie. Rage washed over Aldon like a forest fire, but he gritted his teeth and held his ground knowing the big child could snap her neck in a second.

"Throw that there sidearm in the motor car," Lastus demanded. Aldon obeyed.

CHAPTER 54

ELLIE

Lastus had immobilized Ellie with an arm around her throat. She couldn't move and could barely breathe. She heard someone speak from above.

"Let go, Lastus Slater," the voice said, "or we'll shoot."

Lastus let go, dropping to the ground and whimpering. Aldon moved swiftly toward where Ellie had collapsed. As she looked up she saw two guns sticking out of an upstairs window. One was real, the other, obviously, a toy.

"Shoot that man, Mommy," piped a child's voice.

"Get up, man, don't cower." Aldon jerked Lastus to his feet and grabbed the front of his jacket. He marched him into the sheriff's office, and Ellie followed. Aldon aimed Lastus at the cot in a cell and closed the door with a clang. He stood watching the young man until a woman carrying a baby in her arms came down the stairs with a tiny girl clutching her apron. Without a word, the woman handed Aldon a steel key. He locked the cell door, touched the brim of his hat and handed the key back.

"Ellie, this is Phil Oate's wife, Cathy." Aldon smiled in a way that told Ellie he liked the plain looking young woman standing there.

"How do, ma'am," the mother wore a flowered wash-dress. "This here is Calvin," she offered the baby, and Ellie took him, not knowing what else to do. She'd never held a baby before, but in a moment he melted into the crook of her elbow and she relaxed.

"This here's our Constance," the mother nudged the child forward. "Say, how do, Ma'am." The child stuck three fingers in her mouth and lowered her head.

"Hello, Cathy. What beautiful children you have. Thank you for rescuing us." Ellie said.

"You're most welcome," said Cathy. "I'm sure you'd do the same for us." She turned to Aldon. "Where's Phillip?"

"He's looking for this fellow's brother." Aldon said. "I heard you call his name, you must have seen him before."

"Yah! The two of them have spent a night or two on our cots. They like their likker a bit too much. Did you eat?" Cathy asked sweeping her gaze from Aldon to Ellie.

"Yes'm, and so did that bushwhacker there, don't let him tell you any different," said Aldon.

"I'll have to cook his supper later, anyhow, but he's not too picky." Cathy tilted her head and looked into the cell at Lastus who sat with his head down and his hands hanging between his knees.

"I've got to get gasoline for the automobile. "Ellie would you like to come or would you rather stay here with Cathy and the kids?"

"You're welcome to come up to the living quarters over the jail, but you'll have to excuse the mess. I never get caught up." Cathy's voice was wistful.

"You don't have any help?" Ellie asked.

"I do all right." Cathy shifted the child to her shoulder and patted his back.

"Is there something I could do while I wait for Aldon?"

"Well, I am running out of diapers and I happen to have the laundry water heating out back. If you could do some washing I could red up the dishes, nurse the baby and get him down for a nap, then I'd come outside and help you. That's a lot, though, isn't it?" A blush crept into Cathy's cheeks, as she looked shyly into Ellie's eyes.

Vera had taught Ellie how to use the washing machine at home. It would be no trouble at all. Aldon walked her through the jail to the back door and opened it for her.

"Where do you suppose the washing machine is," she asked him.

"We need to see that the county gets them one," he said. "We just never thought about it."

Ellie heard the upstairs window slide open. Cathy barely had to raise her voice to be heard. "Take the stick and fish the diapers out of that big galvanized tub where they're soaking and throw them in the pot, hanging from the tripod. I already put in the soap flakes. Stir them around then take them back out so you can rinse them in that other tub. That's cold water, so you can wring them out before you hang them on the line.

By the time Ellie finished the difficult chore, she almost wished she hadn't offered to help. She sat down on a rock and rested against the rough bark of a tree. When she woke she was being gently shaken by Aldon who leaned over her.

As he pulled her up, she came out of a dream about him. She slid her arms around his waist holding him tight. In that moment, there was no past, no future, no diapers and no criminals. The ranch and their jobs no longer existed —only Aldon and Ellie. She looked up at him and he touched her waiting mouth with a tentative finger then kissed her. Everything in her received his love as freely as he gave it.

Neither moved until the back door to the jail house opened and the sheriff came out.

"Hey, what's going on!" he said in a mock, gruff voice. You can get arrested for that."

"Can't you see we're doing the washing?" Aldon said. He threw back his head and laughed with joy.

"The wife appreciates it," said Phillip Oates with a chuckle.

"Where's Furstus?" Aldon asked.

"In there with Lastus," said Oates. Where did you suppose he would be?"

"Calvin's asleep Thanks for washing them diapers," Cathy said coming out with the little girl.

CHAPTER 55

ELLIE

A week later Bill and Shirley arrived on the train. Ellie drove the flivver to pick them up and Aldon took the spring wagon for the things they had brought from California.

When the train pulled in they walked to the platform to greet Aldon's brother and his wife. Bill stepped off first, then they heard a voice saying, "Don't let me get stuck in the doorway," and Bill helped a woman down the steps. Aldon stepped forward and clapped Bill on the back.

"Judging by the luggage coming off, it looks like you're planning to stay a while," Aldon said.

"I am here to stay, man." Bill grabbed Aldon's hand and pumped it. "Is this the flapper you been telling me about," he said as Ellie stepped forward. "She sure is a looker, but don't tell my wife I said so." Bill's wife smiled and laid a hand on her roundness. Her husband put an arm around her as if he were holding her up.

"This here's the newest Mrs. Leitzinger. Oh, we got married a year ago, but she's still my bride," said Bill looking at her fondly.

After Aldon helped load the spring wagon, the other three got into the flivver with Bill at the wheel and the two women in the back.

"Look there, it's still light enough to see the snow on the mountains." Bill said as they got going toward the mountains. "Boy, this road is rough. When they going to grade it?" he asked Ellie. He went on without waiting for an answer. "Maybe I'll apply at *county* maintenance so I can make a bit of extra income. I could keep up the ranch and do that on the side."

When Bill had parked the flivver beside the barn, the occupants walked up to the house together. On the back porch, Ellie pointed out the new electric refrigerator. Bill looked over the coats and jackets on the outside wall and remarked. "It's so good to be home. Now that little tyke of ours will be a natural-born cowboy just like me and my ancestors before me."

Kate and Seraphina met them in the kitchen and Aldon introduced them. The Solanos came in and Bill shook hands. When Nancy and Molly arrived Ellie's grandmother and granddad came too. Bill looked a bit surprised. "Wow, we got a houseful, ain't we?"

Shirley needed to rest before supper so after introducing her, Bill escorted her up the stairs to the bedroom Molly directed them to use. When he came downstairs, Ellie took him into the dining room so he could talk to Signor Solano. She imagined it must seem strange to him to ask for a job on the old homestead where he was reared.

"Come in, Mr. Leitzinger, Welcome home, you too, Ellie." Aldon was already sitting in a dining room chair. Bill gazed up at the painting of the mountains on the wall behind it.

"You like the painting. You probably saw the ones upstairs, my Lia is a great artist." Signor Solano turned toward the painting, then turned back again. "We're happy you have come, you and your lovely wife.

"Name's Bill, Sir." They shook hands. "I brought Shirley home to foal because whether it's a boy or a girl, it belongs here."

"I could not agree more." Signor Solano hid a smile. "My dear wife is also expecting the stork, as you Americans say. We talk about going back to Italia, but although she is in good health, I will not risk a long sea voyage. I'm afraid when we arrive at our country home, we will have much renovation to see to because of the war. A faithful few are still there. They took care of the vines the best they could, but the villa was used for a hospital and the cellars for a prison. It is an old farm, so we will work hard to restore it, but we will come back to America sometime, too. We especially love your ranch. It has made me well and brought my beautiful wife such happiness." Signor Solano sat back in his chair. "I will be sorry to leave and I wish to take away a vision of a thriving ranch, so I am glad you came home. Best of all, like our farm in Italy, it will remain in the family. We will be here at least another year, so we will help a little, with your renovations, Si?"

CHAPTER 56

ELLIE

Ellie wore her green chiffon to supper in honor of the returned Leitzingers. After supper, she changed into the trousers Nancy had given her and her boots and Stetson. When she, Molly, and Kate finished, she walked out the back door to breathe in cool air. The moon spread its white glow over the fences and the barn. She should have been exhausted after all the excitement of the past few days, but, she felt exhilarated and restless. She was glad she and Aldon weren't enemies anymore, but now they would go their separate ways, she with her grandparents and he to take over Bill's job in Hollywoodland so he could send money home. She knew, though, that he would find peace in working with horses. A sense of loss washed over her. What could life possibly be without Aldon? The answer came: without Aldon, it was nothing.

"How about a ride in the moonlight?" Aldon came out of the house pulling the screen door closed behind him.

"I'd be delighted," she said forcing herself to sound cheerful. If these were their last moments together, she wanted him to remember her as a strong woman, not a fussy feminine chit who would cry and embarrass him.

In the barn, they saddled Chief and Susie Q and decided to allow

Sunrise to follow along. No need in leaving him so that he would whinny for the mare.

He cupped his hands so she could use them as a stirrup. He boosted her into the saddle. Ellie had no idea where they were heading. She just wanted to be with Aldon. When the road became a trail, she fell back and let him take the lead. Looking at his straight back in the moonlight she gave a sigh of thanksgiving. If there was ever anyone, anywhere, that she wanted to be friends with, it was Aldon.

At the beginning of the trail that led to the warm spring, Ellie pulled back on Susie Q's reins and the horse paused. "This is where we got kidnapped," Ellie said

"That's all over. You're with me now." Aldon half turned in the saddle to look back at her. His eyes locked with hers.

She tapped the mare's belly with her heels. *Yes, she knew she was safe with Aldon. He'd protect her with everything he had in him.* When they arrived at the pond, the well-trained horses waited for the couple to dismount before they began to graze.

"Do you ever feel sorry for horses not being able to lie down to sleep?" She asked dropping the reins in order to ground-tie the mare and dismounting.

"I never thought about it," Aldon said as they approached a fall of boulders at the edge of the spring. "Their knees lock, you know, to keep them upright. Would you like to dangle your toes in the spring?"

"Oh, yes," said she. "I've heard so much about it. I always love the water."

Aldon steadied her as she sank onto a big rock then he knelt to remove her boots. He looked at her socks, then bravely rolled them down and took them off.

"A work of art!" He lowered his head and kissed the top of her foot. His eyelashes tickled and she sighed. When he looked up at her, the reflection of the moon caught in his eyes and gave them a shine like that of a sweet and vulnerable child's.

"*Oh,*" she thought. "He truly loves me. He loves me as much as I love him." Warmth spread through her entire body as peace filled her soul. She sighed.

He drew her to her feet and lifted her. Her arms slid around his neck as she snuggled against him with her head on his shoulder. Heedless of his boots, he walked into the water. It soon crept as high as her waist. In the midst of her cascading emotions, she heard an inner song she had never heard before. Overhead, the stars swirled like dancing angels.

"Ellie, Honey," he said, his deep voice resonating. "Do you know that I love you more than life?"

"I know," she answered breathless. "I'm so glad."

"Why?" He asked.

"What do you love about me?" She questioned him ignoring the fact that he had asked first.

"Your eyes, your hair, your long slender limbs, your smile, your sweetness, your sense of humor, your excellence in everything you do, your kindness, your courtesy, your willingness to be a servant to all"

"Stop!" She said, laughing. "That's enough!"

"But none of that matters. It's your soul I love."

"How do you know?" she asked charmed and receptive.

"It's the way I'm made. Once I give my heart, it stays where it belongs … until death do us part."

"Maybe we'll never die," she said.

"My love for you will never die, because God put it in my heart. He wants you to be my mate for life. Would you consider that, big-city girl? I don't have a lot of this world's goods to offer, but I know I can make you happy."

"Yes, I would consider it." She pondered, holding her breath. She then made him wait while she counted to ten. "Yes, I've considered–I will be your mate for life."

"Yippee-e-e," his voice rose into a triumphal yell that echoed off the boulders. They had come to a deep place in the pond and Ellie felt her body grow light as if she would float right out of his arms. Aldon stepped into a hole and began to sink. There was nothing either of them could do, he lowered her into the water in time for her to stand on the bottom She lifted her face to his. He bent his head. His mouth touched hers. They stood immersed in each other until her whole body was tingling. She wished he would hold her like this forever. She opened her eyes and saw over his shoulder that cloud sized green lights wavered over the peaks. She knew it was the Arora Borealis, a sign of God's blessing on their union.

EPILOGUE

The same Sunday, Pastor Rudd performed the marriage ceremony in the church in town. The entire community attended. The bride wore Nancy's creamy satin wedding-dress decorated with imported lace. She carried a small Bible borrowed from her own mother. A silver dollar from Grandmother and Granddad nestled in her bodice, and tiny, blue ribbon- rosettes held her veil at her temples. The groom wore a Western suit and a new pair of tooled boots that Ellie's grandfather had brought him from the store in Chicago.

On Monday they loaded their horses onto the train and began the long journey to California, making plans as they went. Ellie knew that her family would soon follow, but she and Aldon would find a two horse ranch near-by and they would all continue to be a family. Maybe someday, they'd go back to Colorado, but that was a long time off.

www.ingramcontent.com/pod-product-compliance
Lightning Source LLC
Chambersburg PA
CBHW030743110726
47900CB00008B/2429